The Numb and Me and Green Trainers

The Numb and Me and Green Trainers

Euan Sutton

authorHOUSE®

AuthorHouse™
1663 Liberty Drive
Bloomington, IN 47403
www.authorhouse.com
Phone: 1-800-839-8640

© 2011 by Euan Sutton. All rights reserved.

No part of this book may be reproduced, stored in a retrieval system, or transmitted by any means without the written permission of the author.

First published by AuthorHouse   08/09/2011

ISBN: 978-1-4567-8686-1 (sc)

Printed in the United States of America

Any people depicted in stock imagery provided by Thinkstock are models, and such images are being used for illustrative purposes only.
Certain stock imagery © Thinkstock.

This book is printed on acid-free paper.

Because of the dynamic nature of the Internet, any web addresses or links contained in this book may have changed since publication and may no longer be valid. The views expressed in this work are solely those of the author and do not necessarily reflect the views of the publisher, and the publisher hereby disclaims any responsibility for them.

to my turnip

Foreword,

by Betsy MacGregor, M.D.
and friend

Euan William Sutton is at once an ordinary person and a far-from-ordinary person. On the one hand, he has a spectrum of interests and aspirations that are typical of the average, decent citizen who takes out the trash, cuddles his children, follows the news on television, and likes to go out with his wife for dinner and a movie occasionally. On the other hand, he has a remarkable depth of wisdom and insight that both sets him apart and also at times contrasts glaringly with a knack of getting himself into extraordinarily uncomfortable situations.

As is true for each of us, there is light as well as darkness living within Euan. It is the very condition that makes us all uniquely human. Yet for Euan, each of these two qualities is so inordinately strong that the contrast between them is not only unnerving, but sometimes seriously alarming. It is as if two opposing forces are at war over which one will claim the allegiance of his soul. If he could have it his way, it would be the light, Euan is clear about that, and for much of the time, he manages to be one of the smartest, funniest, and most loving human beings living on this planet. But despite that fact, the dark has the power to periodically rise up and overtake him and drag him away to a cold, foul dungeon where, for a time, he can't be reached by anyone, even those who love him the most.

After being investigated for years by a succession of competent (and sometimes not so competent) psychiatrists, Euan was finally diagnosed as having schizophrenia. Yet his intention in writing this book is not to focus on that dread disease. He is not attempting to give a clinical account of being a patient with such a serious psychiatric diagnosis, nor to provide an in-depth account of his personal experience of living with the condition of mental illness. For Euan doesn't see himself as someone whose identity is defined by being mentally ill. Like other people living with chronic conditions such as diabetes or asthma or even cancer, he knows that illness is an experience you have; it is not who you are.

What Euan *is* doing is offering us the opportunity to meet him as the whole person he is and to see life through his eyes. He tells his story the way he lived it, inviting us to feel what he feels and to think the way he thinks as he rides the crests and troughs of his one perfectly imperfect life. The result is a full-blown, pull-out-all-the-stops immersion in the epic adventure of a fascinating human being who is living his not-so-easy life as fully and as well as any person I've ever known.

Prologue

I knew from the moment Terry put the Latino guy's head through the window there was going to be trouble. I knew he shouldn't have done it just for calling me a white pussy. In fact I knew he shouldn't have done it at all. They say you can choose your friends but not your family. Well, Terry was not family and I should have known better.

When would things stop getting worse. Crack, an elbow hammered my jaw. As I was hunched over on my knees, out of balance it didn't take much for my torso to twist, falling forward my face hit the smooth tarmac with a thud. A knee in my back, my head being held, my left cheek was grated to and fro in a limited range of motion.

My head was hit again with another crack. I made an effort to turn my head to the left where I saw Terry grappling two guys, one black, one Hispanic, both large, but he could handle it. Smack! It was fucking Terry striking me, accidentally, as he flailed about like a man fighting for his life. I knew he loved a scrap but was I missing something here?

I managed to get to my green feet, turned to look over my left shoulder to see who had been giving me a good hiding. I saw the man for a second but my eyes went straight to the shiny silver object with a black grip poking out of his jeans. He spat out the words, "ready to die motherfucker"?

Was this the final lesson? Was the Numb's work nearly at an end, driving me towards its greatest moment, the tour de force in a rather mixed bag of ups and downs? Was this the answer to the question of what growing up was for, to die in a tough hood in Jersey City?

The Numb and Me and Green Trainers

Growing up, in to what?
I felt that life, I mean the function of being alive, should have been relatively clear-cut. Us kids, as we grew up were safe and nurtured, loved and blessed when we began, right? Well, I assumed yes. I was treated to a privileged start, working parents, togetherness and a sister who protected. I was unaware at that stage of growing up the factors that surrounded my process. I went to my local comprehensive school where I was in trouble more often then not and didn't shine. The rift in feeling simpatico with the world, the shift in my process of viewing life, began there.

In this paradigm cool possessions ruled and I was certainly their servant. So the question was, did I have the right Stuff? In a word, no.

Oh, don't get scared off just yet I'm not talking philosophically here, we're not warm and stretched yet. I'm referring simply to the quintessentially important items, none more so than name brand flashy sneakers that define you at ten years old, Stuff. An abstract notion to anyone who did not live that very moment in my newly acquired bright green trainers, expensive, therefore at least impressive to those who shelled out for them if not by a committee of the coolest kids in my school. I took a deep breath, hoping that this would be my moment. The bright Kermit the Frog green shoes would hopefully be sufficiently cool to mark my initiation in to the elite. My heart raced, I neither smiled nor grimaced too hard. I couldn't pick my head up to survey the eyes of the purveyors of cool. All I could see as I stared downwards were a pair of daringly green trainers.

Then problems. My world collapsed, I jaundiced, a nice color to match my feet as the juvenile jury morphed into jeering jackals, pack-hungry waiting to feast and devour me in derision.

I was standing there, mortified by the result of the social selection. There was an immediacy to the situation that shone like a new penny but my head was floating in an intoxicating mist as my green feet were glued to a mire of shit. My green trainers, now a bright beacon of my sub-status, may have been the catalyst for exclusion, but if it hadn't had been them, it would have been something else. They catapulted my inevitable alienation forward and as I turned and walked away, my heavy heart lurched towards inquisitiveness and awoke a sharp jabbing pain from a side of my brain previously undiscovered. A nagging shadow had been born, that shadow was a sense of numbed restraint. I was like a body, numbed by a voodoo anesthetic, still and silent to the outside world but inside a tumultuous sea of flame and fire beat against me. Starting at my feet the sensation surged through my body, to my head where there was now pain. My first taste of exquisite humiliation, fierce and chaotic as it swirled inside, gave no outside tell. I had discovered a part of me that may have lay dormant from birth or was born that day. That part of me, the control cipher now undeniably as real as my pain, would be known as, The Numb.

The Numb had questions that needed answering about this debacle, and so became my champion in the quest to find the inequity of this situation. Images popped in to my mind that would have evaporated in to a sinking mist of low self-esteem. I was unaware of the Numb's motives, but for now I had two choices: as a dissident, the Numb letting me control rage as a mechanism for truth collecting, or as a coward, fading away as a follower taking scraps of undignified residual praise as a non alpha pack outsider.

So back to the matter at hand, with the courage garnered from this pre-pubescent epiphany, who must take the blame for the shoes?

Me? Should I have known more about Stuff, been more self-aware? Was I doomed from the start 'cos I lacked that innate essence of cool? Was it the fault of my parents? Had they paid more attention to the trends and fashions of the young in my stead, they could have foreseen this green shoed disaster, far too perilous for me to anticipate in my bubble of innocence. Was it that my whole genetic line was cursed with a hidden un-cool chromosome? Maybe.

So, playing the blame game was getting me nowhere. The Numb led me to ponder if I could ever have been in control. The Numb early on was a meandering presence. Hints came more often than answers but within the silhouettes, shapes started to appear and the divergent populous of the school became clear to me.

Sporty kids, they had found the golden ticket in to the Chocolate factory, the back stage pass to social etiquette. This sense of pre-destined genealogical prowess played out with their Pearl dropped parents; mother and son and father and daughter bathed in a cess pool of their own importance.

Some kids were average. These Play-doh humans urging the elite to mould them in to their image were left to the mercy of a system already shaping up to be far from nurturing and encouraging. And then there were the rest. They got it worst. They were invisible and only recognizable by their poor selection of Stuff and an apparent smell of urine.

It was as simple as that.

Divinely ratified coronations of the sporting heroes took place all in plain view of the executioner's blunt axe, seen endlessly hacking and slashing at the self-esteem and spirit of those who did not make the cut. So who was that masked butcher of childhood dreams? The Numb and I had seen the beast unmasked. And sadly this amorphous villian had many heads with many faces.

An answer to the Numb's first question had been reached; as it stood I could never have been in control.

My decision not to be sifted and categorized by such a flawed system started that day, and the pebble was dropped in the ocean. Would that action reach the other side of the world?

Well, not right away.

� ✧ ✧

The next stop for me was a trip to the local grammar school. I didn't fit in at the comp anymore, if in fact I ever did. It may have been the green trainers, it may have been that I was weird; it may have been the unexpected arrival of the Numb. I needed to see if the lessons I learned about class were unique to St. Joseph's Comp or if this was pandemic. I was going to have to challenge the system. At St Josephs the only way to differentiate myself from mediocrity was with sporting prowess. I knew I had failed as a sportsman, so what could I use as the gauge for class inequity on a larger scope.

I figured that a feat of academic wonderment, dazzling the teachers at the Grammar school, would be enough to prove academic elitism existed. I would endeavor to score off the charts with my studies and realign the universe for the curtain twitching moral mediocrity.

"Well that explains why he can't kick a ball, the lad's a genius"

"Oh, I see, that's alright then".

Well, I failed the entrance exam. So that was sports *and* academia down the swanee. Elitism as it stood seemed to be so close one could nearly grasp it but the dream of running my toes over the soft grass of Elysian fields was a million miles away. I didn't want to lurch from one failure to the next, proving not that there was this awful tyrannical machine at work, rather that I was just useless.

My quest was already getting a little mixed. I started wanting to break down the social barriers with an incisive stake through the heart. But by this stage a part of me wanted to find something I excelled in; proving my independence was not a by-word for just being contrary without context.

I was given the option to go to a private school in the English countryside. I felt that I could shake free the tattered vestiges of state school education and enjoy the clean, antiseptic air of private school. The wooded promenade, flanked by tall trees standing to attention as if to welcome me, led to a wonderful Georgian building. I was truly a foreigner to these shores and was in need of the Rosetta Stone to comprehend this new world.

Either mum or dad dropped me off at the bus stop. We were taken the thirty-minute ride to school in a succession of dilapidated coaches that unwittingly revealed the shabby side of this new adventure as if the veil had slipped. The drivers were a touchstone of misery and bitterness; it was no wonder then that the school turned out to be a fully paid up breeding ground for pseudo-criminality, whether you were good at anything or not. Sure, you could be sporty or academic but that wasn't where the real action was, the real juice; the litmus test for social acceptance was violence and aggression and cash.

Things were in a state of flux and the embryonic Numb made me realize my first truth; money or the lack of it contributed to social hierarchy. The clique of cool parents from the Comp with their equally cool children were now subjugated to the role of yesterday's news, a part of an underclass which now unequivocally existed.

From early on at my time at Stonebridge I was given a gift I had not seen before: acceptance. There were us guys who got on the bus together, and quickly developed a bond, a friendship that would be tested. Stonebridge was dissected in to six houses, but there was no sorting-hat to find common character traits. We all seemed at first to be the same.
"Punch him; go on punch him in the face."
"What?"
"Go on knock him out, or we'll kick the shit out of all of you"

The Numb and Me and Green Trainers

Fair enough, we had no choice, we had to fight, but this somehow seemed fairer than exclusion determined by what color trainers were being worn.

It would have been easier had they not always paired up best mates to fight against each other. This was no fun, but I got a reputation quite early on as someone who would fulfill the requisite amounts of violence to fill the cool meter. Plus I always felt that Thomas, a hardheaded Czech boy I rode the bus with, allowed me to get a few more digs in than I deserved. Why, I don't know. One day, one of the really cool older kids said he was my cousin. Fuck knows why, it made no sense at all, but it did gift me what nothing so far had: respect.

Random acts of aggression were so commonplace; they went hand in hand with this so-called respect. Once, I punched a big kid square in the jaw on his first day of school, because he assumed too much and failed to obey social standings. I punched him cause I wanted to. He could have hit me back, but didn't. Maybe he was shocked that a kid half his size had punched him to protect his locker. Whatever he thought, there were rules that had to be obeyed.

My acceptance of violence was now a defining factor; I'd found my niche and with social stigmas coloring outside the lines, anything seemed possible. These were the kids of a higher social class and my first hand experience showed that only one rung up the ladder and things were already getting bloodier.

One day I was asked to "fuck some guy up". He was in the year above me, but he was *me* in my green shoes, a dork. He stood no chance against me, especially with the social backing I now pulled. I strode in to the other

kid's common room, making a tribal taboo. Walking straight up to him I felt the pressure of twenty hungry eyes urging me to make my move, so I smashed his skull against the floor. I stood him up, beaming, the jackals looking onwards, I looked in to his eyes and saw a big white gash appear where his hair used to be and then in a matter of seconds blood spewed from him.
I picked him up and ran him to the sanatorium. I was disgusted with myself.
I belonged to a club, but I started to find the "Be Cool" membership fee a little too expensive.

During all this however, things really started happening. I made my way on to the rugby team without being very good and my exposure to drugs went from zero to total immersion. At this stage I was angry, violent, but bizarrely very anti drugs. Guys from the bus would palm me eighths of hash between classes. I frantically dispatched these little parcels into the nearest toilet bin or bush with the conscientious fervor of a spy making a dead drop to nobody.

I was straddling the fault lines. I was getting hints from some teachers that there might have been a chance for me in the world of paying attention and learning but choices concerning my future needed to be measured and advancements had to be made. I felt the subject of contradiction. On one hand the target of inertia being swaddled in fetid bloodied bandages, on the other a sense of being pulled mercilessly onwards. The people I was interacting with were like incidental flashes, devoid of meaning, empathy or soul, yet held an occult attraction. I had learned that at grass roots level, school life in England was oppressive and with the middle class private school came a lawless snobbery of those who wished to ascend further than maybe they could, but would still have plenty to sneer and look down their noses at. But the violence and turbulence was rife due largely to the removal of superficial fashion minutia.

The Numb allowed me ways to voyeuristically and lasciviously bathe in the blood, sweat and fear of other parents and their children in their mutual struggle to be relevant. I pushed quite hard at the boundaries of common decency. Despite the anger and violence, I felt it was all a sham, a pantomime of what it would have been like had I had been brought up in a rough council estate around the country.
I was fighting on a near daily basis, had ready access to drugs, porn and booze, some of my friends were Satanists, we cut ourselves, we bled, but I never felt any of it.

We had a competition one day where one lad and I were put to the challenge of using one fingernail to scrape and scrape at the skin on the back of our hands until one or the other of us conceded.
The look of nausea on the challengers face when I intensified the digging after he conceded revealed a rare fear, despicable yet addictive, as I yielded to the Numbness. This was a brave new world where I was either the voyeur or the touchstone for depravity.

The dream of invincibility was broken one day. The homeward bound coach journey was a pleasure, I was popular, and it was a time when we could all group

together, some of the younger ones, some of the older ones all sharing the experience of living within a violent school.
When we got off the bus however, we were the weak; targets for the tough lads from the local comps, the ones from broken homes with nothing to lose.
There were two suicide attempts by people I knew at Stonebridge. These guys, if pushed far enough wouldn't have given two shits about taking one of their father's 12 gauge SG shot carts, loading them up and unleashing some of the churning hell spawned from years of institutional abuse on anyone who found themselves in the wrong place at the wrong time.

When I was younger at the comp there were people who would go on to be rough, wielding knives, fake guns and peddling small amounts of drugs. These working class pit bulls were to be feared, or so we were told. But feared by whom? Us? We were ritualistically being kicked senseless; we were being taught how to strip down and reassemble a Cadet GP assault rifle in classes, we were being hung by our ankles naked outside thirty feet high windows, we were being drowned in rivers, we were tough little shits.

Why was I, at the epicenter of this playschool violence, so afraid of the world I left behind? I was still standing there with my green trainers on, now with the Numb. Unable to reconcile the fact that the person I wanted to be had been violently achieved and the person I had enjoyed becoming I knew I wanted dead.

So as we ascend . . .

* * *

My mother worked for a distinguished lady whose being coursed with serious imperial blue blood. Mum was her cook, cleaner, driver, and personal assistant and was on the clock most the hours the day would bend to. Mum was paid a very poor salary and in essence was bound to a life of indentured servitude. This offered Dad, Joy, Mum and I a place to live: Monastery House. This manor house was a unique place and the only place I ever called home.

This was problematic in my understanding of class issues as they related to me. My home broached social boundaries in a rather unique way. Mum put in the hours, often being treated like an old fashion skivvy, yet I had the opportunity to grow up exploring a house steeped in history, tradition and beauty. The owner of the house may have been as the queen of hearts was to Alice but I was in Wonderland.

Rooms that were secret and forbidden, nooks and crannies in the vast acreage of land were all explored. Sledding with dad on sheets of hardboard down perilous slopes, trashing the croquet lawn with a cut and shunt motor cross bike; I was given summers full of insects, laughter and experience.

Here the Numb was not, or at the very least lurking like a patient terror, continually being thwarted by the radiance of adolescent sunbeams.

A lot was taken for granted at Monastery House. My education, emotionally, was already advanced by the age of ten; yes, I had my green trainers to live with but

I was learning exponentially that life and people's lives stretched far beyond a monochromatic palette.

"Mummy why does that man live with another man?"

I think the answer that I was given was that my neighbors on the estate were *special friends*; in hindsight this was a fair euphemism for explaining homosexuality to me, a life form, bereft of any tangible sexual experience, but who may have accidentally rubbed the dormant nub of genitalia against a post, car seat or whatever, and thought of honeyed mischief without words, context or meaning.

It became normal to see men hold hands and kiss and as I got older hear reports of a whole catalogue of sexual exploration including an endless barrage of fucking, sucking, felching, snowballing, transvestitism and a smattering of S and M, CBT, et al. This was all conducted with an orgiastic fuck you to the world, in the potting shed, in a bush, wherever. I learnt what cottaging was by thirteen whilst my peers weren't even able to grasp two men being sexually intimate. I had known a man die of AIDS whilst the guys on the bus never talked about the existence of it.

In a time of such labored expressionism, concurrent with such soaring freedom, society had become so crystallized over the issue of homosexuality.

Erasure and the Communards were uplifting. Frankie was setting us up to be shocked. There was an overriding mystery to me that existed in the rigidity of the gay

The Numb and Me and Green Trainers

and anti-gay construct. I saw through all the smoke, generated by the friction of voracious name-calling and near violence, as rather disingenuous. Neither party really gave a shit about each other's differences; they were too busy doing what they wanted. The lunatic fringes were laughably deliberate in winding each other up and whilst the anti gay extremists demonstrated their ignorance in a more physically aggressive way, it was a redundant tactic in an unwinnable war.

There was for the first time a deconstruction in class warfare. Rich old elephants supported young kiss me Kev's in a symbiosis outside of traditional family values and class. Was sex at the centre of class distinction?

Sex, which brings me back to the disintegration of invincibility I felt on the school bus coming back from Stonebridge.

A new guy, who wasn't worried about the sphere of influence that surrounded me, decided he would teach me a lesson. At the back of the coach he pulled down his fly and pulled out a handful of pubic hair and forced them in to my face. This action seemed to transcend all social hierarchy, dissolved all social boundaries and was revealed in its full grotesque perversity. Most of what went on at school stayed at school, a gang mentality that offered a sinister institutional self-protection on a daily basis. Having the musky taste of a handful of pubes thrust upon me contradicted all reason and was beyond my understanding. The Numb understood this injurious revelation but I needed action. When I say action I really meant retribution.

To make a long story short my father intervened and things got very real very quickly. Dad ensured I was in the safety of his car whilst he cooled down. The trap was set and this rat was going to get his comeuppance. The new guy finished that week at the school, then requested a transfer to another school in another part of the country. This was a reminder that we were toy soldiers, playing, testing life, a far cry from perilous consequences that could occur outside of the faux-violent incubator.

This experience showed me the toxins we wielded were more bile than poison.

I was privileged to be well-liked by the lady of the manor, the boss of my tireless mother, who happened to be on the board of directors of one of the foremost public schools in England. I wanted out of the life at Stonebridge, a couple of phone calls were made on my behalf and I was on my way to the entrance exam to sit amongst the social elite of my country.

However, I was oblivious to this at the time. I had huge failings in the maths and sciences department due to years of neglecting my studies. My reasoning skills and my English skills were still sharp enough to enable me to pass the exam; this coupled with a weighty conversation from on high, got me an offer to Langley School.

Wow, how things had changed: the local comp, the local lads, the private school with its private problems, would this public school allow me to go public with my cumulative and accelerated awareness of class and the nature of standing alone?

I had been given two clear chances to be an individual and due to various circumstances found the edges of some of my abilities.

As I moved up the ladder, subterfuge and politics climbed with me.
The comp taught me that you were mostly out of control in determining your fate.
Stonebridge taught me if you wanted something you had to fight for it.
Between living at Monastery House, with all of its bizarre goings on, and Mum and Dad's company booming, surely now I could escape the Numb. But what I failed to realize is that you can move in to a different world, but you cannot transfer earned respect or experience, coolness or dorkiness; once again you are a clean slate.

So how do you survive a hostile environment, completely disenfranchised?
You either became the Machiavellian Prince or you slipped in to mediocrity. I however held on to a trump card that nobody else knew existed; it was time to reawaken the Numb.

* * *

At Langley I was a misfit again. Nothing would prepare me for how public and explicit class dogma was and how it would be rammed down my throat.
Without the Numb I feel I could never have lasted my first two years at the most fiercely hostile, cold, elitist boot camp for our captains of society. I was awkward looking, skinny, often called rat boy. The absence of a title in my parent's name, or six zeros behind an integer made me a hard sell to my peers. I had come from a rough place where violence won the day. Langley had

an institution of fear that could attack individual psyche in a far more insidious way than a punch in the face. Social exclusion equaled death. Once again the being great at sport was a must for social dominance. There was however far more room to move into excellence: You could be a fledgling academic, play beautiful music or be gifted in art.

To my frustration I felt I slipped through the cracks of all the above. My worst fear, mediocrity, was looming down on me. If it wasn't for the dark malevolence of the Numb, a force that my new peers could neither understand nor believe in, I could have drifted endlessly on the coat tails of the alpha cats.

I got swept up in wanting to be everything these kids were, knowing that on the back of my Stonebridge experience I could never have been a trusted member.

You see, the closer you got to the top, the criteria for a person to be accepted as one who deserves life, became very stringent.

As a piñata is hit again and again, eventually the belly bursts and the attackers are rewarded with the innards, momentarily salivating over the sweet entrails of violence and destruction, in the same way a few jovial swings and *you too* could be beaten in to submission, paying the toll at the gates to the elite dream. I had the foresight to see I could never be welcomed, guts in or out. So, I subsisted through the first two years with much imitation, toadying and groveling. Monastery House, my family and the Numb enabled me to get through somewhat intact.

And then something magical happened.

I was in the upper fifth form and despite not being sporty, musical, academic or rich, I was getting some

The Numb and Me and Green Trainers

attention from the young, horny sixteen year-old girls who bravely or stupidly decided to join our ranks at Langley. This attention somehow gifted me the one thing I coveted; respect.

I was a usurper, plain and simple. Some of the young girls farmed out to complete the social fabric of elite young adulthood, were finding *skinny rat face* attractive. Not just that, but more desirable than the free range cocks who strutted around obviously more eligible than me.

I had some power again now. A misfit, outcast and alone, and would have been left alone, but for the sheer desperation of the alphas adolescent libidos. With emasculation on the other end of the sexy see-saw, my inclusion in to the inner circle was reluctantly permitted, in the vain hope that some of my desirability would rub off on the now disarmed prince charmings, dying darlings of pre-lust life, and tilt the see-saw to their vain favor. With the war of hormones raging, those given the cold shoulder by the fairer sex became the lost generation of should-be eligibles, but not.

The crown prince of desirability at Langley pulled me to one side at a poncy party and said to me,

"You know, you're a good looking bloke"

I said, "O.K."

I was now *in*; and just in the nick of time. The Numb was ready to explode in me like a poisoned appendix.

I had cracked another social circle, once again with a heady formula of sex and fear. I had control over at least some of it, whereas others did not. Consequently, their fear of exclusion and social death became reality. And as the morgue filled up with lost souls chilled into submission, I had an urgency to put this newfound glory to the test.

And so there was an interlude in Long Island.

✹ ✹ ✹

I think it best to describe why I was there in the first place: Firstly, I was taken on a family vacation to Orlando, Florida. On one of my last nights at the resort I walked past a swimming pool and saw two girls about my age, 16, squirming around. How exotic these tanned athletic creatures appeared to me, then a heavy New York accent chilled the balmy evening,
"So who are you",
"Oh, me . . ."
"You were looking at us right",
"Well sorry", head down, about to make a bolt out of embarrassment's way,
"Hey don't run away we were just bustin' your chops"
What the fuck did that mean?
"O.K. then"
"You're from London right"
"Well I just live south of . . . yeh I'm from London"
"That is so cool, Beatles, Zeppelin, awesome"
"I guess"
"So I bet you like Thomas' English Muffins, right?
"What?" different lingo to the norm, definitely.
"I don't know what you're talking about, sorry"
"Holy shit, he's never had one and he's English"
Sinking, needing inspiration, arms skyward, just be cool,
"Want a Coke?"
"Sorry we can't, we're leaving tomorrow. This is our last swim"

"Oh, shame".
The risk of making a dick of myself was lost in the intoxication of this very foreign, very once in a million chance to pioneer transatlantic shagging at Langley. This would provide another wry smile to add to the amassed pile of irony-ammo to fire in desperate, nauseating, shit eating moments of soul-jeopardizing lip-biting when listening to the Langley alphas continual one-up-man ship.
"Want to exchange numbers"
What were the odds of anything happening from this? Fuck odds, the rest is history.

I was waiting at La Guardia airport, sixteen years old, from nebulous southeast England somewhere.
Bianca, by this stage was expecting an eighteen year old from London called Will. Scratch that, Wil with one 'l', sounds cooler, good.
When preparing a major international visit to a girl you don't know under a bogus premise and identity, I think it's fair to say that fate would have to be shining on me with an intensity requiring SPF5000 to avoid getting severely burned. With sunscreen left unpacked things were most likely not going to end happily ever after.
Redefine culture shock; whatever is high on the Richter scale, this one was a needle-breaking whopper. It was hard enough to distance myself from the vile stench of Langley School that I was cloaked in but I also had to operate and maintain a living-breathing lie that was so flawed it stifled me.
I was paraded around the local spots, Dairy Queen being the first. Here people thought how cool it was that I spoke funny. I was taken bowling where the assorted

gang of strangers, were amazed that I wasn't completely shite, how quickly I picked up the concepts: ball, lane, pins and throwing. No finesse, just cave man style hurling, but it passed another superficial day, avoiding any challenges to my brittle artifice.

As for my budding relationship with Bianca, she by default became the object of my affections. The other one in the Florida pool had collected a bona fide college stud in the interim. Not good. So Bianca, the high school senior, to my hunky college freshman façade, was unlike any girl I had met before. This would prove problematic. I think she smelt a rat from the start. She would had to have been deaf, dumb, blind and simple to not be at least a little unsure of my shallow cover story that would disintegrate in to a morass of lies and counter lies just to stay plausibly buoyant.

Despite all this we had a semi intimate relationship that prompted a stark warning from Daddy, or Big Mikey as everyone else but Bianca called him.

"Hey, Kid",

"Yes Mikey",

"See this, Son",

"Yes Mikey".

"It's got your name on it, but you don't never need to see it again up close, unless you hurt my princess in any way".

When really weird shit happens right in front of you, it can have a dramatic effect. When that weird shit for the sake of argument is having a 22mm bullet given to you with such thought and taken away again with equal consideration, what could I do but look down to see my trusty green shoes and know the Numb was in full control of the surreal, almost cool nature of getting

The Numb and Me and Green Trainers

my first death threat. We went from that to throwing around a football in the back garden.

It was fair to say that I was getting along far better with the family than I was with Bianca, who would allow some strained fumblings as we watched Beavis and Butthead together. She was clearly growing weary of my now implausible pre-trip legend.

By the third bowling outing Bianca was absent, citing ladies ailments. No skin off my nose, I could barely stand her by this stage, day three into the trip. I felt pleased that I was being taken out by Big Mikey's brother, the Dentist. He got his name by performing ad-hoc dental practices to unsuspecting sharks, prizing open their mouths and extracting the hook that he had firmly planted there. The Dentist was a big bastard; he came across like a big paternal Grizzly bear to me. His acts of dentistry were not to illicit coos and wows from an audience, proving his manliness; he was just cheap. He thought fellow fishermen foolish for letting these hooks slip away in the gobs of one of the most feared animals on earth. Different strokes . . .

Whatever his monetary modus operandi was in fishing mode, here at the bowling alley the horn of plenty was overflowing. He snuck me beer, cigarettes and most valuably dirt on Bianca. He put it best, "Don't worry pal, that girl is stuffed full of more shit than a Thanksgiving turkey". The Dentist could never officially break family ranks but I was overjoyed with his sentiments and the gifts kept on coming.

So wearing a NY Islanders hockey jersey, feeling ridiculous but happy, my smile faded to a sucked lemon pucker as I remembered tonight Bianca and I were to straighten things out. With a supersaturated bullshit solution ready to crystallize all around me and with no exit strategy I had to just let things unfold. Not an easy proposition when remembering my discussion with Mikey.

The door opened, feeling desperately anxious, I stood up. As I stood there Bianca entered and before a tirade of crap could fly out of my mouth she shuffled forward a couple of steps, strange, no not strange when a tall handsome twenty something was hot on her heels. Apparently she had driven in to the side of his vintage Mustang in Port Jefferson. While the blah blah banalities of their unplanned collision were being rattled off, I took a deep breath seeing how Bianca and Brad were bumping in to each other as they talked, how their eye contact was a little too long.

Great, I could come clean, lift the lid on the whole stinking lie I concocted and flush it down the nearest outlet pipe to the Long Island Sound; home to bizarre fish and crustaceans, not for the faint hearted. Anyway, I could come out of this the victim. Cowardly, yes, but who could blame me in this situation. Bianca was far too busy discovering the mysteries of Brad to ponder the mysterious workings of my calculated, experientially dogmatic sense of truth collecting. Experiment: go to Long Island and lie; having to lie for the higher purpose of soaking up life that would have otherwise been out of reach with nothing to suck up but the stagnate solution of middle England truth. I came clean to Bianca. I had lied about my name, age, schooling and would now be going home.

P.S. Your dad can't kill me, you broke my heart with Brad, hope it's true love. Sponge nearly full; there was one last surprise in Long Island.

The Numb and Me and Green Trainers

I was invited to a going away party, partly thinking I was going to be killed by Big Mikey, I went not realizing how wrong I would be. Mikey and his wife Julia were really supportive and I went to a cool party on the beach. Beer was being poured down my throat with equal quantities of Zima, but the thing that happened that day would change both me and the Numb forever. Somebody passed me a one hitter packed to the brim with weed. I puffed, got high, was drunk on an unfamiliar beach in Long Island, New York, yeah, fuck you Langley, I was cool. But then came the guilt of crossing the threshold, it lasted about five seconds and chillingly foreshadowed what would become quite an illustrious career with illegal drugs.

Oh well, back to earth. The Numb and I were exhilarated from our escapade in New York but experiences were savored only in my private moments, as any mention of such unfettered original fun and outlawed social behavior would be attacked with acid vengeance from the inner nebular of Blue Bloodia.

I felt I was coming in to my own. I was getting some fantastic education from the English department, some of those guys truly inspired me. The theatre department was a constant tribute to the day that took the fun out of art and then laughed.

My face didn't fit, I wasn't all singing and all dancing and the teachers tried too hard to force an academic slant on the subject. I only chose theatre studies to see if acting was cool but more importantly to avoid real school work. Must have been something to do with the national curriculum, exams and the like, but who needs educated actors? Pretty meat puppets can do just fine can't they? Strangely, in the Department's eyes I was a lazy, moaning, arrogant shit.

The social rifts were larger than ever. The men and women of the local comp thought we were all soft foppish tarts. Most people of the right social class, our lot, saw the townies as peasant folk, thought the janitorial and maintenance workers were shit, but I noticed something else going on other than the occasional half-arsed skirmish by the doner kebab van. Some of the alpha cats at Langley wanted something that they could never have officially, a touch of the wild, an organically planted toe on the wrong side of the tracks. To have a street savvy, local weed middleman as a friend, leant some serious credibility to them as they saw it. You see, they may have been at the top of the pile but the chains of boredom, and shackles of anonymity trapped them just as they do most kids, top, middle and bottom.

These captains of industry wanted to experience, albeit in a much-protected way, all the things the last five years of my life actually had been, warts and all. I never pandered to this though. I kept the underground identity of the Numb as sacrosanct, so I played along: wanting to hang with Fizzi, 'cos he was a little bit street and could roll the perfect joint, etc. Remember, it was the pioneering Alpha cats that discovered this breach in social convention; a drug induced armistice in the war of the classes.

As the son of a working class man, a man who would often pick me up from school in his sign written work

The Numb and Me and Green Trainers

van, I'm surprised it took these young gentlemen so long to figure it out: what I was, where I came from and all that I may have been privy too outside of Chelsea, Brighton and or any other place caught within the fine bubble of a champagne dream life.

Most of them were blind fools, swept up in the immediacy of serving themselves extra helpings of all that protected society children could get their hands on. Many of them had achieved feats of pill popping, and party politics that far exceeded the Numb and my conquests thus far. I was afforded a chance to breath in the luxurious irony, that while my current peer group jostled and juggled who had fucked who, who was left in the stiflingly incestuous pit and who scored drugs from who without getting too far out of the safety of Daddy and Mummy's social safety net, I had a fully paid up Union of Scholastic Excellence scholarship to attend to and play, free from their shit. I imagined my future of liberal experimentation as a wholly sun filled dream of sex drugs and rock and roll.

Well, in two years from that fantasy I would be vomiting blood on to a cat piss stained carpet in a Queens basement apartment, with one semi functioning window just out of reach, overwhelmed by the obnoxious television set, volume max, Macy's day Parade mocking me with red and white candy caned artifice, ticker taped dirge. My crime: plagiarizing their color scheme in my grime. The blood red and china white in my flesh vacuum nozzle and the confetti of kitty litter, completed the Me Day degrade; no sun, just the steely blue refractions from the Numb's prism.

I wasn't hell bent on proving the Langley boys as fakers; they were just playing the card that their cosseted life dealt them. But as my path towards self destruction moved on, various truths fell in my lap.
I had learned my lessons of class growing up in the UK and now it was time to fuck-up my A-levels, have my best friend shag my girlfriend, very unceremoniously I may add, and digest what had happened to me in the last four years. This was aided by lots and lots of drinking.

Whether I wrote this stinking drunk or crispy dry I surmised:

If we're all being led up the garden path, towards the big pointy pyramid, you'll find that with every toff saying he thinks working class people are beasts of burden on society, you'll find a working class bloke saying all rich people have it so easy and don't understand what real people have to do to survive in this unfair cruel world, with all those in the middle reflecting both arguments upon themselves, why don't more people want to take a chance and shake things up a bit.
I choose a few years of sex, drugs and boozing Stateside to beat this Chinese finger puzzle 'cos life isn't fair; to beat the trap all you need to is relax.

If the sum of your life
Can be negated
So easily so crudely
With a tone of indoctrinal drone
Your passion sated
By nothingness

The Numb and Me and Green Trainers

Then death has become you
And you
Honour
Your purgatorial home

See you later, planes to catch, chance to see if that stone I dropped all that time ago did make it across the pond. But before that as the big cog grinds slowly on, still a few minor jobettes to attend to. So . . .
I made my way up to London to participate in an extemporaneous debate about euthanasia or some such uplifting topic as part of the process of my selection for the scholarship. These U.S.E. scholarships were quite rare and prestigious, awarded usually to the male or female antithesis of what I was. The scholarship was designed to send a child from one social elite to a comparative social foreign elite to perform some perfunctory ambassadorial duty.
A chance for me to entertain the foreign sports hierarchy with a dash and a flash of organic wit and heroic strength, exhibited by the previous year's scholar from Marly College.
"I know it's not a cricket bat son"
"Well coach, just toss me the ball and I'll hit it, you can call it what you want"
With that the hero stepped up to bat with a gentlemanly poise, grabbed a baseball bat held it like a cricket bat, and turned the onlookers indolence in to incredulity as he smashed the ball so far and deep that immediate sporting reverence was achieved. Well, our hero knocked their smirking view of cricket for six, social job done.
It was the same with American football.
"You know this ain't rugby son".

"Just give me the ball coach and you can call it what you want".
As he smashed and clattered his way through a host of defensive players desperate to make up for the ball smashing event and cripple the rugby playing buffoon, they lay in his wake defeated, amazed that an Englishman was capable of such ferocity.

Oh how I looked forward to be faced with such measures of men.

I was serving out my time at Langley School with the Headmaster increasingly bemused by how such as a mediocre nobody like me was looking the firm favorite for the Scholarship. The Headmaster had a son at Charterflat, a school of some stature, who was an all rounder and certainly a far more obvious candidate for such an important scholarship thing.
Well none of this mattered. I knew I didn't have to be good at anything really, nor likeable or easily controlled for I had a trump card to use; our beloved Class structure. You see I had a benefactor who not only sat on the Board of Governors at Langley, but also was heavily important within the Union of Scholastic Excellence. To top all this she was a true blue blooded aristocrat with Imperial letters after her name.
When the Headmaster had to ratify consent for me to go on this holiday abroad, or as it was officially put 'representing my school', following the whip hand of a class trap he had unfortunately been dragged in to, as a middle man unable to ascend beyond his station, unable to defy upper class wishes, he must have felt humbled

The Numb and Me and Green Trainers

and infuriated by his mediocrity and impotence in preventing me getting a free pass.

Or he may have just accepted it as a natural course of events in a system he knew far better than me.

This is a timely reminder about being fair in life, letting life be fair or otherwise. Here I was receiving this scholarship through mostly covert channels, and it felt normal.

I was not surprised. The Numb and I had come too far to be surprised by the inequities in the effort to reward ratio in the battle of the middle classes, the flesh production line so desperately afraid of mediocrity. Any input from above was gospel, with the lower classes standing in as punching bags to use and deride as needed.

Yes, I with the Numb could see this, notwithstanding my vulgar and shameful ass licking to some members of my social group; just enough to have a visceral understanding of their movements and spy onward ever learning more.

The scholarship was obviously in the bag but with my apparent uselessness holding up a big red flag, how could I avoid being seen to have beaten the trap in the process of being myself? You see you can get picked up in your dad's work van or a Ferrari but in social war only strategic targets could be found in the fray. I escaped notice and was never truly a target for attack because I was never really on the inside.

A member of the Aristocracy had leapfrogged me from working class to Scholarship boy, so nobody saw me coming.

Euan Sutton

My time to recreate myself had come again with the trip looming ever closer. The Numb was working hard wading through the muck and fishing the bile oceans of social inequity. The sun was at my back but as the earth moved the seemingly endless highway became rugged terrain. My eyes were rendered little more than slits as the morning star blinded me; I would have to accept my dark crusader, as I did not know yet the depths I would sink to. I was taking deep breaths with all those experience molecules floating around getting sucked up making me light just for a little while before it all started again.
Wincingly, I dug; I was surrounded with beauty and the profane:

Dig said the man
No not in your word-hoard
That fackin maintenance line on the M25
So he dug and found nothing,
No relics no bones,
But he did find a rare jewel sparkle
It was not in the ground
It was running down his face catching the light of his mysteries
The teardrop fell in to the hole,
THUNK
And the man looked up
And said I've given myself back to life
I am a jewel maker now, my riches will be born to those who feel,
Bullshit back to work said the Forman
You gone crazed
The man said

The Numb and Me and Green Trainers

No but I think for the first time I can tell a hawk from a hand sore.

I purged, got ready for a trip to North Carolina, yes sir North Carolina; that's where I was to spend the next year of my life. So I rushed out and bought some blue tinted contact lenses, they made your eyes look quite cool in a freaky way. It was my time to freefall in to the vastness of experiential life. I had in essence beaten class in the UK and I was a in a state of frozen shock as to what things were like in the South, Deep South that is.

✻ ✻ ✻

Got on the plane, arrived the other end without incident, plain sailing. The members of the International Club at Postville School greeted me at the airport. All the traditional welcomes and pleased to be here stuff was rattled off, and from early on I was impressed by the attention overload thrust at me.
The place was spectacularly beautiful. I arrived at the end of August and had never been kept awake at night with the sounds of nature buzzing, ticking and bumping against the immediately acknowledged necessity, the bug screen.

I woke up the next day, went to the communal shower block and grimaced. The room had a bank of hand wash basins following the left wall, all perfectly normal. I got to the end basin, looked right to see a puzzling arrangement of porcelain receptacles, unusually low to the floor, with flimsy three feet high screens separating the five units. Could these really be the toilets? I must mention, and I don't know if I'm alone on this but I am extremely delicate in regards to shitting anywhere other than my hallowed, magazine not other people strewn, home toilet. I attempted one sitting, just to see if I could be manlier about the facilities but the sounds of farting, plopping and squelching, wiping, shuffling and groaning was a little too much to bear. The locals who were more used to such occasions would happily converse over the din; I couldn't, nor could I face a year of it. So my first objective was to wander the campus in search for what was in all probability the least used toilet. Due to the urgency of this situation I found on day one a lovely, quiet, fully closed off place. It did enforce a sense of premeditation about one's bowel activities; timing was essential with a mandatory curfew in place.

I returned to the dorm to have a shower, another adventure where none should have been. Taking one bottle in to the shower I was delighted to see a large shower room, fully partitioned off with slightly mildewed curtains. It was mid shampoo when I noticed an escalation in the energy levels of those around me. Was I about to have a Prison-esque welcoming to Postville? No thankfully, but what occurred was bizarre. Three guys, later known to be Chad, Luke and Miles in unison said,
"Man these fuckin shits stink."
Interesting local color, I know.
"Yeh, fuck these stank ass curtains."
And with that they attacked all the curtains pulling them off the rings in a frenzied state. Within seconds no modesty could be saved, I stood naked, the new boy,

The Numb and Me and Green Trainers

English no less, watching as the nude figures of these strangers, arse cheeks, balls and dicks of various shapes and sizes were now flapping around, their owners with mad, gleeful looks on their faces, blissfully unaware of any sense of shame with bundles of shower curtain material in their arms. They squeezed all the material into the bathroom bins, then returned to their respective shower heads beaming like conquering heroes, heads back, faces in the water, legs wide open, very manly; I had to face the facts that here I was on day one laid bare, literally, to my peers. I would have to see if the Numb and I could find solace in some subterfuge, if the excuse of cold-water shrinkage was not accepted. What I failed to realize was that nudity was commonplace for these guys. They had played American Football and had been living together for years. So with every locker room jaunt and countless communal daily ablutions, came familiarity with each other and de-sensitivity to being naked. So in spite of my newness I may well have gone unnoticed. My nudity must have acted as an invisibility shield to those conditioned not to stare in the shower, because as soon as I was clothed I couldn't stop getting positive attention all day. After such a weird morning, with no time to regroup I was unprepared to deal with getting flirty eyes from nearly all the women and high fives and earnest welcoming from the guys. Don't get me wrong, this attention was great but I hadn't even had a chance to swap my green trainers for more suitable footwear yet.

Hold the phones; was there no class structure as such here? Did it not matter where I fitted in on the hierarchical ladder? I hadn't been asked about my sporting acumen yet although I'm sure assumptions had been made that I would naturally fill the shoes of last year's Wunderkind.

Well of course there was an institutional class structure there, and although not obvious from my initial meanderings, I would find one that matched our own, with an insidious twist that made for a far more incendiary battlefront. The brittle mask of over zealous political correctness failed dismally to hide obvious unhealed wounds carved out of the racial divisions still endemic to this part of the world.

Hopefully, as an outsider, there would be something I could learn from this extra dimension without picking at too many scabs.

It was assumed that I hailed from the upper echelons of British social life to get this gig in the first place, so, I sat back on that one initially and allowed people to think whatever they wanted to.

One of my earliest memories of Postville was nearly my last one there. It was at Breakfast and people would have to queue in a waiting area until we were marched in. Things seemed very formal which made me feel a little uncomfortable so with the assistance of a well-positioned fruit bowl, I felt a little, 'Is that a banana in your pocket or are you just pleased to see me', humor; a must for setting the tone at my first breakfast. The Headmaster, Billy Peeps, wanting to get a glimpse of the new scholar made a bee line for me as I was mid gag. He was far from impressed.

The Numb and Me and Green Trainers

It actually caused quite a furore. The insane way an immature but innocuous visual comedy bit was pounced on with such ferocity revealed a self-fuelling anger engine of epic and biblical proportions. I had just unwittingly brushed against a *majorly* sensitive button.

It occurred to me that the rich elite in the Bible Belt may be all for hanging, or was it hanging on to the true beauty of their artifice by one godly string, because the devastation a six inch banana caused, threatening their way of life like a giant pair of scissors waiting to snip at the tentative tentacles from heaven, or as I saw it the highly strung twine, holding the whole bag of lies together. Anyway, the situation required trans-Atlantic appeasement.

I reconciled to the Numb that I would only be able to come out and play behind closed doors or at the very least behind a shiny shimmering distracting veil that careful observation, truth collecting and Numb consultation would create.

It seemed I was a social warmonger, unable to avoid conflict in my raw state.

I was mulling this over when I fell to my knees, not in the throws of a religious transformation spurred on by my morning's fruited sinfulness, nor was it an emotional realization, an epiphany if you will, revealing something or other. It was a lot simpler than all that. A block of ice the size of a football had just crash landed on my head. I thought that someone had been dared to drop this icy projectile on the new kid's head, for the obvious purposes of testing my metal, or skull. This whole episode could have become fighty, and bitey and mean. Was I going to have to scrap my way in to social

recognition, as a dorky outsider? Hey, maybe I would have to play the social games I thought this 'now you see it, now you don't' town would spare me.
I opened my eyes; Mrs. Cartwright was crouched down beside me with her daughter Annabelle. Annabelle was considered the most eligible catch in the pond, her mother was politically powerful both in the confines of the Postville school and the larger Postville scene. Annabelle's dad, Mr. Cartwright owned the franchise of a very successful new car dealership that enabled the family to have a big house, nice life and all that.
My eyes squinted open.
"You got the prettiest eyes," said Mrs. Cartwright in a refined delicate southern twang.
I smiled at the beauty of the situation. My eye color was fake, contact lenses, and I could have been crippled with the convergence of the twain, my vain gloriousness and the new term's defrosting freezer's offering, the ice ball. But no, I was demanding the attention of some of the power players on the scene, on my first day. Intimate concerned moments no less, were our first to share. As it turned out the whole incident was an accident, really. I had the genuine concern of Jorge; one of the most popular young men there, and all his friends immediately became mine as part of his guilt shedding reconciliation package; although it was with my head, what a way to break the ice.
Sorry couldn't resist.

With the Banana Incident resolved, Annabelle, Jorge and Co onside, Mrs. Cartwright taken with the beauty of my artificial soul windows, things were looking very good. Maybe I was starting to get a little control.

The Numb and Me and Green Trainers

Then I caught a glimpse of a young skinny girl sporting a soccer uniform, the sun was shining in my eyes but I could pick out her white blond hair blowing in the gentle wind.
The Numb went in to spasm, the sense of control I felt was premature and in one moment I realized the year may not be plain sailing after all.

The rest of the day was spent trying to keep up with the pace of change that just being in this new environment pressed upon me. I would see people scurrying here and there and attempted to scurry with them. I eventually conceded to the overwhelming rush of being in an environment totally alien to me and so natural to everybody else. There was something exhilarating about being so out of step with the flow of life. I'm sure the others were not moving as quickly as it seemed at the time, nor was I wading through treacle, but with familiarity there was purposefulness in their movements and I had neither. So I went back to my dormitory, walking past open doors, seeing people unpacking vast amounts of belongings that transformed their neutral cells into mini-homes. I nosed my way down the corridor, saying hi to the ones who caught me prying, staying silent to the backs of heads that didn't notice me. Some people had more: knick-knacks, flags, mugs, stereos of varying size and expense, jumbo sized bottles of laundry detergent and a variety of other stuff. From my initial spying I could already see that some people were more prepared than others and some rooms were more colorful and energizing than others. I felt sad for those people whose rooms seemed lacking and then I got to my door and looked in. I was fully aware that with the distance I had travelled, and having only just got there I hadn't consulted a local interior designer regarding my living environment choices, my room would be sparse, but with two partially unpacked suitcases as the only distraction from the minimalist look I wasn't going for, I felt sapped of energy, drew the curtains, laid down in my clothes and nodded off. My sleep was light and I was restless. Again out of step with the hustle and bustle and frenetic first day back buzz, I let the taunting allure of sounds and voices outside my door morph in to a pleasant white noise and then I slept.

I woke up early the next day, found my towel scrunched up on the floor, damp from the day before, but when I say 'my towel', that was it, the only designated drying item I had, so off I went to the curtain less showers, hung my towel up, maybe too little too late but never mind, turned on the shower which to my delight adorned me with gallons of piping hot water. I heard someone else coming, so I quickly made a break for my towel. A fluffy, warm, and summer fresh delight it was not. My dank, almost stringy looking towel, hanging on the hook like a condemned tramp on the end of a noose, would certainly not have the advertising execs joyful but it was all I had so with no choice I wrapped it round my waist. The material was cold, unpleasant and unwelcome, like if you had fallen in a pond on a day out. The only saving grace was that it was still slightly perfumed with the scent of home. I would have several more towel experiences like this, made worse only by arriving late to the showers now luke-warm and if late enough cold. Fortuitously, when all hint of home had been removed from the towel and screamed out to have a wash of it's own, I discovered we had a laundry room in the basement. I learned this as I started talking to my neighbors on my hall, all at about the end of week one.

So I was up and washed, changed and ready to go to breakfast. The trouble was it was about 4.30am; my body clock was out of whack. Due to the time I had anticipated that although I was up at an ungodly hour, I would at least have the shower block to myself, a rare treat indeed when living in a dorm. Bizarrely and awfully as I approached the showers I heard someone else. Why the other person was showering at this time remains a mystery.

The next two hours were torturous. Every time I heard a door open I would stride out of my room to accompany whomever down to wherever. Unfortunately, I found myself repeating this rehearsed shit about eight times to bleary eyed strangers in towels, just awake enough to see me, ludicrously well presented to anyone still bed-heady. I felt like a stalker when I came out to see a bloke, now clothed, clear eyed and wondering why this was the second time he had witnessed this in one day. When I opened my mouth to speak to him any suspicion passed and he delighted in rolling out the U.S welcome wagon to the much-anticipated British scholar. I was taken to breakfast, banana free, then he asked a question that would enable me, that day, to move at the same speed as the others. That question was, "have you got your class timetable yet"?

After having it explained to me what this was, an awful dark cloud descended upon me.

Timetables? Schoolwork? Timetables and schoolwork, unfortunate aspects of the scholarship that I had totally forgotten about.

I was put in some quite difficult classes, which was fine, but there were other classes that I didn't fancy doing one bit. It was a fiasco: Advanced French, touch-typing, Maths and a bevy of science subjects.

I already had my four A-Levels and ten G.C.S.E.'s earned fairly and squarely in England. As for Science and Maths, subjects not thought about for three years and barely even thought about when I was faced with their respective exams, I didn't want to feel fifteen and dumb for a second time, so I decided to make the rules up as I went along. With the GCSE certificates in hand I explained that I had already demonstrated proficiency in these subjects and how it would be a gross waste of time to rehash over things I had already mastered. It was a gamble; further probing in to exactly how proficient I was, would have led to disastrous timetabling consequences; but the gamble paid off. I was now exempt from all the classes I had no interest in, and doubled up on the ones I wanted. I could now fill my brain with cool info given by some excellent teachers and ignore the curriculum all other students had to follow, a deserved place as misfit, picking classes a la carte, already breaking down some walls and a few large rules.

I felt like taking a trial separation from the Numb and shouting out, "Yeh, you had wonder boy last year, reptilian and cold with a tongue to reach in to many cavernous holes. This time you got me, a human with a perfectly proportioned tongue, which makes up in acidity what it lacks in probing power. I am Brit, true blue and vital who has snuck in here to debunk any ambassadorial sap, collected and saved as artificial amber under a bell jar by the International Club to prove value in this scholarship deal, evidence to break free of inward looking American isolationism."

The Postville institution had sat down at the table with me ready for a game of Go Fish but I had Three Card Brag on offer not caring whether they knew the rules. I had reshuffled the deck, hid threes up my sleeve, no bluffing necessary. Bamboozled and not understanding how I could be so different from their other points of reference they resisted folding early, and anteed up again and again as I won more and more. They stayed at the table to attempt to win a hand, and learn something about me in the process, but they were not equipped to deal with the Numb and me being out there, rigging the game, antagonistic, paranoid and calculating.

I wanted to gorge myself on this feeling; I was pretty much getting everything I wanted.
But the Numb had a plan and was deeply threatened by the chance I had of crafting normalcy without undue edge or conflict. Enter from stage left the anti-Numb: Abby.
Abby shone like an angel. She was fifteen, I had just turned eighteen, but she was not a target of sexual conquest, she was beauty. From the beatings at Stonebridge to the belittlement I felt at Langley and the slew of one-night stands, Abby's innocent friendship took away the pain and absolved me from my tainted life.

The Numb whispered the words *pervert* in my ear preparing me for the chaotic modus operandi, the inevitable dehumanizing process in which I drove relentlessly towards lustful gratification over others feelings, using my past record, viciousness and selfishness, as a template. In an attempt to find unfettered understanding of the social order here, the Numb was prepared to lay Abby's innocence on the alter of discovery.

I was not.

Her purity would not be tainted by me, whatever the cost to the whole experiment. I disobeyed the laws I made, those of ruthless, objective truth finding, and the consequences were mine to bear, and they were fierce. I felt a quasi-demonic urge to self-destruct. Having broken the rules, I tumbled in to introspection, which snowballed in to disassociation of me the pioneer and me the human. Had this decision rendered me a fraudster, or reminded me that arbitrary dogma is death and I could flex once in a blue moon?

Beer and weed to soothe my brain and agitate the Numb.

The Numb and Me and Green Trainers

In order to take pleasure in destruction
You must feel the gears sheer
Lay down as the glass gushes gallons of shards
Taste the marrow in splintered bones
Look in to the inkblot dislocation and say
Deconstruction is something isn't it
The twisted framework of a piece of art
Left only for the salvagers to pick over when
The debunkers start to debunk her
When you're safe in your Numb bunker

Abby was my challenge: To avoid destruction in deconstruction.

❋ ❋ ❋

Quite early on at Postville I established myself as both inept and disinterested in sport, but no one seemed bothered. It was clear that this was not a school that would demand sporting success in order to be accepted in to the social elite. I was doing well enough in my studies to avoid negative press. My favorite activity, the one that seemed to fit me like a glove, was extra curricular and enjoyed by a surprisingly few number of students: smoking large amounts of weed and drinking loads of cheap beer.

One of my biggest surprises, or culture clashes if you will, that I discovered at Postville was the snitch mentality that most people had. The students were actively encouraged to grass up another student for anything at any time. I found this very hard to live with, not just in reaction to the ferocious treatment dished out at

Stonebridge or the stiff upper lip behind closed doors secrecy at Langley, but because it just felt wrong. The act of sticking it to one of your fellow students was called 'turning somebody in'. I just couldn't understand why anyone would take the time and effort to purposefully ruin someone else's day, week, year for no apparent reason. I knew the good Christian superficial façade had brainwashed some people into believing that it was their duty to save a troubled soul by stopping the rot before it could spread. I also knew some people just enjoyed being ass lickers. But with trivial misdemeanors like swearing in the library to whoppers like being out of bounds all being lumped together as collective evil, I heard the grinding of a sinister, manipulative right wing heart, flutter under the milky skin of the establishment. I felt that I had stumbled upon a fascinating glimpse in to the larger framework of American brainwashing of their children. In England we were all kept silent by having it pummeled in to us, here there was a system of controlled fear to shut you up. Children being instructed to spy on their peers, and if necessary make notes to turn in to their trusted guardians, was bad enough. But to sell this fascist horseshit as Gospel was just wrong. It was a cherry picked bastardization of the universal concept of 'Love thy neighbor' that robbed young minds of personal respect of their own judgments and replaced them with fear.

Subsequently, you can see that my chosen activities were neither easy to pull off nor were they to garner some sense of rebellious cool. If that was the role you were going for, Postville School wasn't the place for you. Come to think of it, the School seemed to be a dumping ground for kids who had tried the rebellion routine elsewhere and having been expelled, were placed in an environment where the parents knew it was not just the faculty keeping an eye open to the evil that our children do. I couldn't help but feel their was an oppressive, collective imperative to scrub away the Huck Finn footprints of childhood exploration throughout Alice's Wonderland and beyond, 'cos they were dirtying up paradise, all nicely sanitized and Satanized.

✷ ✷ ✷

Being in the mountains in winter did open my eyes to a majestic natural beauty, not that the other seasons here weren't all equally spectacular, but with winter came snowboarding, and that sounded really good.
The first organized trip was uneventful, a clammy school bus lurching up the side of a mountain, waiting in line to pick up a rental board and bindings, and of course snowboarding boots. I guess the school bus was an acceptable part of the picture but I realized after the first trip that the rental portion of the day would have to be replaced. It was hard to still be waiting in line to pick up well worn bargain basement rental equipment as your friends came in to sight, squeezing the last drop of exhilaration out of the mountain before the no wake zones of the learners slope ended that particular run. It was even harder to actually go out on to the slopes with the equivalent of a beaten up green station wagon as your board, loosely clipped in to green boots, whose smaller shoe cousins can be seen colonizing bowling alleys up and down the universe, and by bindings which resembled two watch straps. Yes,

my set up was un-cool, but it was fitting to the coolness, or lack of, I exhibited on the slopes. My mentor for the day was Jonny, a pal from school. He owned and used the snowboarding equivalent of a Porsche 911 turbo, a Burton Twin with matching bindings and very comfy boots. Jonny said the best way to learn was to jump in at the deep end, I thought why not, so off we went to the top, or was it? I said to Jonny that I thought the mountain looked bigger from the distance, and was surprised about how short the run was. He laughed, and told me that this was only mid-station, and there was a separate lift that went to the top. To back track a little, there are a few things I need to explain. I apologize in advance to any snowboarding pros reading this, I know everyone should know the fundamentals of the sport but some won't. So as simply as possible: At the time I was snowboarding there, you required four basic things: a snowboard, bindings that are fixed fast to the board with straps and clasps protruding in a manner to fasten item number three, your snowboarding boots, sorry no wellies, to the board and fourthly some goggles or sunglasses. The other clothing was optional, but when the wind whipped up in the Blue Ridge Mountains you would wish you had chosen warm over cool.

So that's that for equipment, now on to getting up the slope. At the place we went to there were two-seater chair lifts to take you half way up the mountain then another two-seater set up to get you to the top. Even with Jonny's help, I learnt early on that getting on and off these contraptions was a feat in itself, for snowboarders at least. The chair lifts revolved continuously around the getting on and dropping off points at a rate of about one every ten seconds, and if you weren't in the correct position in anticipation for collection the chair wasn't going to detour from its relentless drone pattern, so it was advisable to be in the right spot. For skiers this was easy, they had both feet fastened to their skis and two poles to assist them gliding effortlessly in to place with the grace of a swan gliding over a pond searching out the perfect place to take a crap. But for the snowboarders, it was a different story. You see with snowboarding you get no poles and if you fasten both feet to your board on the flat you can't move. Well, you can hop around like a mad rabbit and take your chances on a clean lift pickup, despite the fact that you would look like an arse in the process; or bind your leading foot on to the board and use your unfastened booted foot to push you along skateboarder style. This method when mastered was safe, reliable and looked impressive. An amateur attempting this was not that safe, it was still a little hit and miss in regards to lift positioning and left you, and again in saying you, I mean me, looking like the archetypal disjointed member of the living dead except a drunken version with a six foot board stuck on a foot. With Jonny's help getting on the lift, although potentially treacherous every time, became manageable after a few attempts. Getting off at mid-station was the same story: swans and zombies. The difference was, getting off required balance with movement at the same time. Once again timing was crucial; the big wheel keeps on turnin' so with the help of the strategically positioned slope you would attempt to slide down, unbound foot anywhere on the back of the board, down and away from the lift. Many attempts to slide were made, but falling, rolling or something reminiscent of a flailing armed scarecrow surfing was the norm. And if you wanted to get to the top, repeat as stated in the instructions. So Jonny told me we were only half way up, I asked if it would be a good place to start from, he told me yes, if I was an English sissy it would be fine. I could of course follow him to the top. I didn't even have time to think about the fact that I'd never snowboarded before. I think it was a combination of the impish up-curl in the side of Jonny's mouth that could be construed as satisfaction in my decision, the views, or the way the mountain hushed eventually to silence, that suppressed my anxiety. Even at the dismounting station at the top things were quieter, smoother and a lot easier to get off of.

So brimming with confidence I was ready to set off. Jonny thought it would be better for me if I now fastened my boot to the back binding, I said only American sissy's fasten blah blah. He said,

"If you get down the mountain alive with both feet in, it would be a miracle".

I fastened my foot in and waited for instructions. He said, "What are you waiting for?"

I hopped forward and gasped. I did attempt to get five or six feet without falling over but trying was all I had. I hadn't learned to let go yet; fear was as much responsible for my falls as skill shortages. Maybe it was a natural process, as you got better you learned how to be free of fear and get out of your head. I'm glad Jonny had a sense of humor because it must have taken us forty-five minutes to do the ten-minute run to mid-station. But by the time I got to mid-station I felt sublimated and as I looked up I couldn't think of any other way I would have wanted my first snowboarding experience to be. For one reason or another there were several times I went on the snowboarding trips without Jonny, usually because he had gotten in to trouble and was restricted to campus. The down side of this was Jonny was a cool kid and a patient tutor; the plus side was that when he couldn't go, he would lend me all his gear. It was these times that my snowboarding got much better. There was a certain cool factor that possessed me when togged up with all the right stuff that definitely was a confidence booster. Other people seeing me all kitted out properly expected to see something like talent, that in turn spurred me on to improve. The quality of the ride was so much better on the Burton, I felt much safer and more in control than with the rental equipment. It was not long before I let the Numb envelop me at the top of the mountain, switch off my brain and fly. From then on I always went to the top, without thinking about getting off half way up, except just one time.

Another scheduled snowboarding trip and this time Jonny could come, which meant it was the rental gear that week. This was obviously not ideal, but by this time I was hooked and if it was a choice between renting a board or not going at all, the choice was an easy one to make.

So I was at the rental booth being fitted with the best they could muster, handed over payment and reluctantly went out towards the slope. I brought an extra pair of socks with me to provide further barrier between my foot and the well used boots and add a little extra cushioning. I found a problem binding my front foot on to the board securely. The straps just didn't seem to close tight enough, allowing my foot freedom to tilt and rock on the board.

But with the rental line snaking back out the door and my anticipation to get out on the slope, I ignored the problem assuring myself that the bindings weren't that bad, I was just being nit-picky, spoiled by using Jonny's gear so much. As I made my way towards the chair lift, I bumped in to Rose, a girl in my glass who was always good company so we decided to ride up together.

With gravity pulling the dangling board downwards I noticed that one of the clasps holding the binding shut had popped open. I looked over to Rose to ask for her advice on what to do, but when I looked over she was in her own world smiling, so I decided to make a decision on my own. I reached down and grabbed the board with my right hand and released the other binding strap with my left. Now I had both feet dangling down and had brought the board up in to the lift with both hands. At this point Rose asked what I was doing. I replied in a nonchalant manner, "I'm having trouble with the bindings; I'll jump off at mid-station and sort it out". She smiled back as if to validate my decision. As we approached mid-station I reminded myself of the plan one more time; jump down with board under arm quickly to avoid getting hit in the back of the head by the lift. And then came the moment of truth. I jumped off as planned with my board under my arm looking behind me to avoid getting clipped. And then silence. I was in a void, cold and empty. The Numb had taken over the show one hundred percent. I couldn't feel; I couldn't even comprehend feelings, just a sense of being close to the end of my journey. I could see though, I looked up to see Rose crying, but she was always smiling, I couldn't understand. My head nodded down, hey I was on my knees, what was I doing down

The Numb and Me and Green Trainers

there. I felt weightless, my body hunched over, I could see the snow had turned red all around me, I focused on the patternation of the blood, concentric circles, dark red close to me, getting lighter away from me. There was no horizon, no fear, no pain. I was drifting now, and my audio senses, although nearly gone, could pick up low, protracted moans, with an occasional higher note floating for a second like a willow the wisp. My next recollection was sliding, unable to move my head, but that was fine because the stars were radiant and warm, I felt close to them. My thoughts now vagarious, with the exception of specific fondness for my family, I remember the dull echoed shouts from the figures in red around me, "ouuuuttoffffffffffttthheeeeewaaaaaaaaayyyyyyy", "rreeeeeeeeeeessscuuuuuuuueonnnnnnnetoooooooobbbaaaasssssee", then nothing Silence took hold of me once more, no cold, just stars, asking them if I was dying.

Then I was lying on a table, I could sense that it was hard and felt like my head had been bolted down, with the bolt sticking in to the back of my skull.

I remember little else, a trolley ride, an ambulance, feeling colder. At some point in time I had regained sufficient awareness to see that I had no clothes on except my boxer shorts, I could now turn my head but still felt residual pain of the bolt I had experienced. A doctor would later explain to me that my clothes had been cut off at the mountain paramedic station, and that I had been put in a head and neck brace to immobilize that area in case I had spinal damage. After the CT scan revealed no serious organic trauma, I was put in a wheel chair and taken to have my head shaved then stitched up. What an anti climax. I was told by a passing nurse, "you lost some blood up there, but head injuries always bleed more and look worse than they actually are. You were lucky; the other one who came off the mountain tonight in a neck brace won't walk again".

Three hours later I was informed that the most notoriously hard assed, old fashioned, strict Postville schoolmaster was enroute to pick me up. I was in just my shorts; the hospital would not let me take a towel, so there I was with a handful of stitches in my head, cold, exposed and alone.

I don't even think the irony of Billy Peeps, the Headmaster, pulling the old banana in the trousers trick could have lifted my spirits. Numb was off doing something far more exciting and I felt like a boy in green trainers waiting to be consoled by anyone who would listen, but there was no one and I didn't have the resolve to console myself. A few hours ago I had been in the midst of all the hubbub, treated in a way they treat people they think are really likely to die. It is remarkable and dare I say flattering, that all that work is being done for you, to protect your body.

An alarm bell went off; there you are Numb, you scoundrel. You almost let me off seeing the difference in effort that is given in saving your life in actuality, compared to the abject indifference given when you are alive again.

I wasn't going to die, so I wasn't special. I was alone, humiliated and vulnerable, slightly guilty now for making such a fuss for nothing, and there it was.

There were too many people to care about and without medical insurance, the care stopped microseconds after I was non-critical. I was relegated to a member of the lower spectrum, and as I wasn't going to die, it was quickly on to the next patient. I was in essence dead, in any emotional or spiritual sense, to those whose loving microscope I was just under. Had I had been on a better plan, that eight hundred pound chair lift smashing my skull would have garnered a lot more caring, maybe a bed to rest in or a soothing nurse to feed me pain pills. As it stood I was a semi naked boy, cold and disoriented with a pounding head, waiting on a stiff chair for a lift back to Postville from scrooge himself.

Maybe I'd been getting too complacent and this was the push I needed to get normal, appreciate that which I always seemed to be at odds with.

But then the witch-hunt started and there was no turning back for any of us.

✱ ✱ ✱

The senior class was sent off to a 'get to know you now or never' kind of affair. We were bussed up to our cabin accommodations and meeting rooms where we would engage in group activities.
At the end of the last night all the seniors were perched around a log fire, the scene was picture postcard perfect. Our task was to elect various jobs of varying social distinction to our peers. My name was mentioned. I thought, "What's this going to be, an award for near misses?" But no. My peer group, much to the obvious open mouthed horror of our faculty chaperones voted me to be class orator, the individual given the unilateral blessing from their class to voice the opinion of our

collective year's ups downs, successes failures and I guess, our soul, man.
I was gob smacked, delighted and felt that I could actually make some relevant observations of my experience as an outsider to an audience of over five hundred people.

The grimace on some of the faculty's faces should have been enough foreshadowing to the inevitable conclusion of my new responsibility. In any system where social control worked its trickery, an outspoken, non-American would by hook or by crook not be performing the task of class orator.
One of the most fundamental intellectual riddles posed to me at my stay at Postville was the prom. There were so many questions that I had that defied answers. Why would you set up a social gathering where the normal biological imperatives of teenagers were at bursting point, then ban all those fun things like sex, drugs and rocking out at the end of a school year using the argument that fun could be had in other ways; what like telling each other uplifting PC unfunnies or remarking on how well blah blah had matched her shoes with her hair clips. We were kids for Christ sake. What was this abomination? A mock up of how Fred Jr. would have to look, act and talk as his Stepford wife was leered at by his best buds?
Look but don't touch, guys, look but don't touch,
wanna touch, can't
wanna feel her heart beating double time,
wanna slide my hand up her skirt
wanna bend her over, rip off her silk panties and fuck and feast

until all the followers saw I was the alpha,
roaring,
me, me, the fucking king of my stinking country club wife-swapping, sick-note of a life.
And then Fred Jr. recoils; 'I'm very sorry Mr. Blank,
I was momentarily distracted by the beauty of your daughter.'
'Well you're a great kid, why don't you all go out and have some fun'
He slips Fred Jr. something, what is it, a wrap of coke, a couple of hits of X, some acid, micro dots, mushrooms, a hop flask full of Makers Mark, a condom or five?
No, under closer inspection we see a single dollar bill, and if we listen carefully enough, we hear, "have her home by 9:30, this is a little something for the collection plate for tomorrow, our church needs good men like you praying for our families".

And there you have it, purposeful, direct politicking.
No fun.
Prom mission statements should have read:
'We know we can control most of you, some of you maybe, and a few we can't. Those who fuck with us will learn the hard way, how we do things down here.'

The Numb was bored, the wheel of fortune had been so random thus far, and I decided to go the whole hog.

There was one time down there in North Carolina where I felt the Numb saved me from flipping out.

Social tensions had grown between large groups of the kids in my class. I used to get along with everybody. This was no more.

It was a long year of beer drinking, weed smoking, cigarette smoking and dip, but this was also the year that I first tried LSD.

I had this friend called Boz, he was super cool, like a middle eastern Huggi Bear crossed with Marc Bowlan. Cool, just smooth, at least at first. I used to hang around with Boz and a couple of kids from Tbilisi, Georgia, and Ali from Miami. There was also this super rich Asian cat from the previous graduation year, who sat in the backdrop like a fucking thorn in my side. I don't know why, but he was just always there when I didn't need to see him. I think it was something to do with Annabelle and jealousy, oh well. And there was Jorge, a Mexican who's dad apparently owned a couple of tequila companies, was it true, don't know don't care, but it was obvious that the Technicolor tinder box bunch we were couldn't avoid catching the odd flying spark. Boz half way through the year moved in to a palatial home. Remember I grew up at Monastery House, so wasn't easily impressed, but his place was beyond dreams. It looked like Tony Montana's house in Scarface and with one of the Georgian duo almost always in Scarface persona this was a fine dwelling for us hangers on to see what money could buy in the USA.

One day at Boz's he pulled out a sheet of paper and said, "wanna hit?"

I guessed it was acid, but didn't want to ask in case I broke the cool, clove cigarette and Pink Floyd moment we were having and said "is one enough?" Boz laughed, he gave me one.

Well I can recall being really floaty and safe, the Numb kept me continually paranoid, but that was to be expected. The evening was spent talking shit, drinking loads of beer, smoking loads of cigarettes and laughing. The next morning was cool, the whole gang was either eating eggs or waffles or cracking open another forty ounce of Bud.

This was weekend living halfway thru Postville School.

Well, one day Chad was pissed off, I could tell this by spots of Jorge's blood on his white shirt. Jorge had shagged Chad's ex, apparently.

You see I kept one foot in each camp, the Euro lot and the good old boys from my dorm. The good old boys largely disliked the gang from the Morrison dorms and felt the Greenwich boys should stick together. They were not happy with my spending time with a foot in both camps but for a while I was the top dog. But after the Chad/ Jorge thing I had to pick a side. I picked the Greenwich lot.

Miles was my main confidant at Greenwich dorm; he was a good hearted, consistent friend, with a 'South will rise again' flag plastered over his walls.

It amazed me that in such a pious environment the implicit message of the confederated flag with skull and crossbones in the centre, the skull wearing a confederate soldier hat holding a smoking pistol in his skeletal clutch didn't raise any red flags. My reason for such bewilderment in the obvious social control could be summed up in seven words "is that a banana in your pocket?"

Obviously slavery was less offensive than ill placed fruit.

So Miles from Georgia, may have been the best friend I made there. He had a great all American family and the Numb and I related to his compulsivity to alienation coupled with diehard loyalty.

Rob Miller was a handsome silver-tongued Southern gentleman who applied a sense of situational ethics to most things.

Rob's grandpa lived bizarrely close to the Postville School. It must have been on the grounds, at the very least just on the cusp. Rob lived with his grandpa; his home life beyond this appeared troubled in a rather dark sinister way. I rarely talked about Rob's family; I only met his dad once, a strict manicured man, in full control of his beautifully manicured house. This new life Rob's dad had created, half way across the state from Postville had the fingerprints of a surgical separation from the past, and a slight antiseptic waft could be smelt if standing the right way around Rob's dad. I was deeply saddened to see that Rob was to his family, a diseased, non-essential organ, removed to Postville to preserve the healthy life of his new mother in law's family.

Rob had been cut out and thrown away. Daily, Rob crawled bloodied and nasty out of the biohazard refuse sack he was so unceremoniously deposited in to. His permanent wry grin was torturously hiding the sobbing eyes of a child. Rob was damaged, but he was good at golf and good looking enough to consolidate my woman safari hunt team. He offered me the hand of friendship and moreover the shotgun seat in his car. Yes, he drove. He could drive me away from Postville School, illicitly of course, and get me back again.

The Numb and Me and Green Trainers

Through our little soirees I saw some things that took me out of my head and crashed me into the epicenter of my contradiction in finding social truth.

I was in the head of the dysfunctional social elite; Rob drove me twenty minutes away from the school and there were kids, white and black with no shoes on. Rob and I sat awhile, cruised through the derelict slums these people called home till our beers were gone and cigarettes smoked, and then called it a day.

In England I had never seen kids with no shoes, smiling.

I'd been in the heads of the rich too long; mesmerizing me with glitz, I had forgotten what it was like to be poor. The dislocation was exacerbated by the difference between what I thought of poor and what I was witnessing there. I felt greasy and opulent. I knew that the helter skelter would take you further in to poverty if you could shake off the queasy stomach and stay on the ride.

But some of them were smiling; no shoes, dirt caked on their face; that was me at Monastery House, but play not real.

This was real.

With champagne empathy I desperately wanted to feel, but feel anything but shallow, rendering me a second hand emotion junkie.

Numb, you were there right, because it was getting airtight round my neck. The imaginary shoelaces of a shoeless child, destined towards a life of living with class and watching fast lanes, were choking me.

I felt like screaming; give these people a chance to live, before time expires on their childhood downy sunsets awakening a new cold dawn.

"Rob take me away from here now."
"Sure, you okay?"

So I had found an innate truth, I was on a voyage of discovery, but I was growing ever sensitive to the dagger point I was balancing on. When you get close to truth, you also get close to defense mechanisms, suspicion, and headaches like you can only imagine if you know that feeling in the blind fury of a heavy migraine, the membrane, the sac around your brain shrink wrapping, then pop.

I woke up sweaty and unhappy. I felt like a bourgeois fraud.
I was having problems, because I wasn't playing the game, I wasn't getting bogged down in the mire of defeatist cyclical rhetoric.

So time for a new fun adventure that, without ruining for you too much, would become the second most emotionally challenging night of my life.
So there were the guys, Rob, Miles, Adam and Chad. We were all ready to go to Chad's mum's cabin in the sticks and whoop it up a little, to alleviate some of the Postville syndrome. I was by this time a changed man. The elite Southern bubble had burst and everything that was good was now invariably turning bad. This evening it turned really bad.

The Numb and Me and Green Trainers

There is a character in the North Carolina story that I have not yet mentioned, not because I'm saving the best for last, in fact the opposite.

His name doesn't come to me straight away; his impact on my life was such that I felt despite my morose obsession with the twisted, this person was the paranoiac hand in the dark, this person was Fred Wilson. He was true serial killer profile material. He was a large hulking guy, effeminate and passive with spits of anger and venom that would lead to him imposing his physical dominance on you.

He was always in the background, well liked by most people, including me. He came from a wealthy family, again anonymous. One of the things that irked me most about Fred at this stage was that he reveled in scaring the shit out of people by driving too fast. One of the first times I took really strong acid it was at Fred's house, with the guys, and all was well. Fred thought it would be a good idea to go for a whirl in his dad's Jaguar two-seater. Five minutes down the road we were spinning round and round amongst trees and foliage. Remarkably there was no car damage; I guess it was kinda fun until I looked up at Fred who was looking down at me like a God looking at an insect. He put the car in gear and calmly made our way back to his house. The Numb was kicking in to defense mode. The Numb was about to give me space to be educated on the dangers of not paying attention.

So we were in the log cabin, loads of beer, about a gallon of vodka and about the same of rum. We also had LSD; we also had two hot young girls and one slightly older girl, attractive, but for the dire reputation of her promiscuity.

Thank you Numb for the pause to remember Abby before the impending onslaught of toxic carnage.

I had no expectations, no plans, just get high and feel. The passage of time was unclear, there were doors being opened and shut, people dancing, I think Chad was snogging Mary, I was dancing like a wet lettuce at Woodstock, I was sitting down, standing up, in the kitchen, having a drink, having a smoke, smoking a joint, talking to him, talking to her and then things went bad.

Two of the girls came rushing out of the bedroom screaming and making a fuss. When you're high, the transition from super fluffy to barb wire is not instantaneous; when the transition comes it leaves you cold, warm tendrils from your prior good high attempt to probe the cold, offering some hope, they freeze, snap off and splinter on the floor and gravitate straight to your nerves, sharp invasive spikes, forcing discomfort and disorientation.
Come on Numb help me out, but,
"Oh my god."
"What."
"Where the fuck is he, that fucking cunt."
Whoa, things had got very grown up here; *the words* coming out of this attractive girl's lips, while I was wrestling with coherent reality.
"Where is he?"
Mary started to cry.

The Numb and Me and Green Trainers

Chad asked, "what's going on?"
"Just go in there and look." What, shit, what was going on; panic attacks do not hold a candle to this.
"Chad what is it?"
"Where is he?"
"What's going on?" I asked this realizing that all I had to do was awake my leaden legs and walk into the room and find out for myself. Was it the LSD or was it fear that slowed me down?

I stood up and wandered to the door. In the corner of the room Felicity was huddled, whimpering, the girls were mouthing murderous threats against Fred. Was this truth, reality or a drug addled mixture somewhere in between?
Felicity, you know the one with the bad rep with men, no don't even think it; there was a human in pain, oh shit, Numb get here now.

Then I was in control.

"Felicity." She looked up with one black eye and a scuffmark over her other eye; I managed not to wince. This girl had desperately low self-esteem at the best of times but a good heart and I wanted to help her.
"Felicity, come sit up on the bed." She had quite a hard time with moving herself but then again so had I off the couch and we were all on the same shit.
It seemed obvious what had happened after Felicity said how Fred had gotten too rough with her and then left. As I said I noticed doors opening and closing but not much else. Were we all co-conspirators in a drug fuelled sexual attack right under our very noses,

or forced witnesses in an elaborated rough sex game between two people I knew precious little about.

Fred wasn't in the house, it was important to speak to him, that's what happens in the cop shows to determine alibis, guilt and innocence and to move the plot forward.
Nobody wanted to go looking for Fred in the woods in the middle of the night, me least of all, our little car spin showed me how cavalier Fred was with his life and mine; coupled with the paranoia of the drugs, the adrenalin and the paranoia that Fred created, this was a torturous night. And then as if by magic or a quirk of memory loss caused by drugs I was sitting opposite Fred in the bedroom like two gunslingers at high noon. The other guys were either in the room with us or in the next room, the door open. Fred had a gallon flask of vodka in his hand; the vodka was splashed with orange juice, some trick for the mind because taste buds got one hundred percent vodka.

I lurched forward grabbed the juice and took a massive slug. I found it strangely revitalizing, like a tire iron wedged under darkness, with every swig one ratchet turn would happen and daylight would shed light on this fuzzy furry tongued, static morning.
Fred's face was a sight, cherry red lips and heavily lidded, stone black eyes. They looked pale and spent, but I was wary of his unpredictability and knew that the Numb had some how forced it's hand to have me sitting before Fred, intelligence gathering.

Fred was far away. This may have been drugs, drink, denial or some serious psycho problem, but he was distant. I asked him, "so what happened Fred", took a swig of the enormous vodka jug, passed the jug back to him, felt slightly more empowered to get to the bottom of this, Colombo style. Fred would not drink; he just keep saying "what happened", back to me. I took the vodka and asked again, "what happened", took a massive slug of vodka, feeling slightly woozy now and seeing the dawn break, said to the guys, "sorry", as if I was a master safe cracker, failing to break the vault to share the spoils. Had my arrogance willed me in front of Fred that night, could anyone else have done more? The girls, all of them were adamant that no police should be called, so what was this whole thing about?
As the morning drew on and the drugs had worn off, sobriety punished us by erasing any last clues only exposed in mind expansion. I was bowling with the two girls having a coke and a cigarette; the bowling became too much of a trial so we went outside to discuss the night before.

The two girls, who were screaming bloody murder the night before, were now at the most, ambivalent about guilt or blame. The thought of a follow up investigation by the police was deemed completely unnecessary; I mean I had delved so deep last night, surely no new evidence could be gathered. Felicity had seemed to disappear off home and the whole incident just blew over, except for the fact that I saw the threat of Fred Wilson that night and on nights before, I felt a resonance between the night in the cabin and me injuring the boy at Stonebridge.

Nobody wanted to talk about it, none of the people involved; Felicity had a younger sister who from then on after would look at me like I was scum; she was best friends with Abby.

I voiced my concerns time and time again about Fred, refusing to be involved in any of the things he was at. But the problem was he was involved in a lot of things, and nobody else, after about one week of uncertainty had problems with him.
I was disgusted with the good ol' boys; irreparable damage had been done. Now there was just the prom and getting the fuck out of the South.

I wanted to honor the prom in the way I think any human would, get drunk and fool around with the best looking girl that would have me. Well my first pick, due entirely to her spectacular tits and ass, and wardrobe of only thongs was accepted, but due to various pressures I had to pass her over. Then out of nowhere this girl who graduated the year before started showing off in her new jeep. Her name was Cindy, she looked okay, had a rep she would fuck, drink, etc., she had rich folks, right, she'd do. It also held a finger up to convention; out of all the girls in the entire school my pick came from outside Postville School.
Well after some to-ing and fro-ing I got my pick and Rob took my risky cast-off.

We were told no motels, no drink, no fornication, so it went like this: Rob got us motel rooms and beer, I made a bee line for mine with Cindy and Coors, he went off

The Numb and Me and Green Trainers

to his. There I was alone, it felt like prostitution, I didn't know the girl and she was already giving me a blowjob, looking up asking if I liked it, I was oblivious, having a dialogue with the Numb,
"No"
"What, you don't like it?"
"It's alright, pass me a beer please."
I shot gunned a beer, very classy and went on to tell Cindy my evening would be a fucking washout if I didn't get laid.
Cindy was surprised but without further ado parted her legs and we went at it for a couple tedious minutes. Not really worth all the sweet-talk after all.
Rob seemed to have equally good fun with his date, as did a variety of other lads on that wonderful Postville evening. The fallout was huge.

You see, despite looking like a twenty one year old porn star, Rob 's date was fifteen and we brought her home after her curfew. Rob referred to her vagina as the tightest mother fuckin thing he had ever . . . in fact he could barley even . . . we can suppose that despite his attempts he came to his senses, or more likely physics intervened and he narrowly avoided committing statutory rape. Mind you after the Wilson thing, I felt any amount of hush hush was possible.
So Rob was done for, as were about seven others.
We had an inter-school judicial system at Postville called the conduct council. The council comprised of six of our peers, two teachers and a chairman. This is what happens when you construct an underclass; sometimes they come back and bite you in the back. Here we were, the social elite of the school having our fates decided

by the entire green trainer, rat faced boys and girls of our class year.

There were six expulsions quite quickly, one after the next. Rob was expelled because despite no prosecution in law, the council felt that taking a fifteen year old girl to a motel room, was probably not to play guess how old I look in the leather thong and shiny cherry lip gloss. Rob was dead in the water. Two weeks before finishing high school, no high school diploma.

This was the problem for all the guys dropping like flies; unlike me they hadn't already graduated with qualifications in England.

So it came down to me, I was stoic in that I refused to rat anyone out, even if it meant expulsion, blah blah blah.

But the Numb had been busy. My sister during the conduct hearing was a guest of the headmaster. The Dean of students Bobby Smith took me in to a private meeting, moments prior to the conduct council he was going to chair. I left that meeting well scripted.

I was also not an unkind person to the social underclass; they too were my friends. One of the most notorious social climbing straight as an arrow creeps came knocking on my door one morning during term, telling me how he had just swallowed enough pain medicine to kill himself, I helped him that night, he lived and as fortune had it, he was on my conduct council.

But what way could any negative outcome make me suffer?

If I got expelled, so what, who would care, well who would care in that really weighty way you care about terminal illness in the family? The answer, Lady Millicent Sloane CBE, therefore the expulsion was always off the table.

I felt washed out. I had broken free of the social confines which gripped some of these third generation Postville school boys, their lives were devastated by their expulsions, but mine was not. There was something they could take away from me that could cut deep through the muscles, sinews, bones into the marrow and I never saw it coming. It was a 'tour de force' rug pulling by the Numb.

I was permitted to stay at the school acting as a gardener, cleaner or assistant in any other practical jobs that needed doing in preparation for graduation day. All this I thought was quite cool. Sure I wasn't with Boz and the boys partying by the pool but I wasn't Rob, having to go to his dad to explain himself.

When I wasn't working I was restricted to my dorm. One day, as I walked back to my humble abode after cutting grass, I was stopped.
"Will you sit down with me?"
"Sure Abby."
"Well, you know that thing with Rob?"
"Yeah, I don't really want to . . ."

I sat down next to Abby and I felt consoled by her soft words and the radiant floral gift of her existence. She was a compliment to life, a secret, majestic yet humble. I felt sullied and ashamed, unworthy of her kindness. She asked me,
"Do you want to talk about it?'
"I'm sorry Abby. You must think I'm . . ."
"I can't believe that when I saw you earlier that night you were on the brink of having so much trouble come your way."
"You looked beautiful."
"So did you."
"You know Abby that I would have taken you but I . . ."
"What you did with that girl . . . I wanted to be that girl."
"I couldn't have done that to you."
"Really, you could have . . ."
I was without words; this was the circle complete; a fiction, a fantasy of a perfect union if I didn't have my old pal Numb on tow. I loved Abby, I loved that life protected her from me, and at the end of our year knowing each other we were strolling through Elysian Fields directionless, infinite and honeyed, yet false and distant, a protected prism of a life we couldn't have.

She kissed my cheek, I fizzed and popped like an unsullied kid again, but turned to her and said, "I'm sorry", smiling, not knowing if I was crying.

Back to the grime and punishment. Just when I thought I had evaded any real punishment, glowing from my brief encounter with Abby, I received word of the true

The Numb and Me and Green Trainers

measure of Postville's vilification of me that cut me to the quick; I was told I could not be the class orator.

A glum, stumblebum, I got hauled up by the English department trifecta.
"It's just too inspired, he couldn't have."
"Are you sure this is all yours?"
"In thirty years of teaching I found a student to validate my decision to teach".
"In all my life I've never met such a disgrace, you're lucky we're not involving the police".
So I tantalized some, some with my pen some with my tongue; for splendid oration was now banned, cunning linguistics' meant nothing and fucking bureaucrats kept me barred from the Shakespeare competition.
The Numb, like Richard III, liked the murderous romp. I was Foul and prolific, digging through social circles with my runty spade, finding much muck, a lot on top and below, and now I couldn't spill my Numb to my classmates and assembly; this would be how my Postville world would end, not with a bang but with a tinkered-with whimper.
The headmaster read out "will the devilish young Englishman collect his diploma", Thank you Mr. Peeps.
Abby gave me a mixed tape of love songs; Bobby Smith, I'd be seeing you in a few weeks staying with Lady Sloane in the UK with us, thanks for the help.

New York was next, after a brief stint in the UK.

The guys from the South said don't go up there, you'll probably get shot, nah, that's just ignorance, that'd never happen to a young innocent like me, would it?

✤ ✤ ✤

So it would be fair to say that my stint back in England was a stopgap. Well, I am aware that the importance of my family, their role and impact on my life has thus far gone unmentioned. This is largely due to the weight of selfish force that had built up behind me, driving on like a juggernaut desperate to deliver urgent cargo to an unknown port. The cargo was my cumbersome head baggage: the Numb and me. Whirlwind lifestyles can become the norm very easily and with a support like the Numb beside me it was very easy to acclimatize to environmental extremes, lusting after meaningless goals at a furious pace. At this stage in my life anything sub sonic left me feeling nauseous and dizzy. I had to move on, so I moved to New York City aged nineteen.

I knew nobody in the city but I was being housed and fed by a tie in from Postville. Chad had an uncle who lived in Queens. When I got off the plane at J.F.K. it was Steve who picked me up. He was a big bloke, which I found very reassuring, knowing that I would be facing this new challenge with such an obvious protective figure in my life.

It was very generous of Steve and his nationalistic Irish-American wife to give me a place to stay, as Molly was heavily pregnant with their son Sean. I later found out that the six hundred dollars a month, paid by my mum and dad, may well have assisted in their spirit of generosity.

From where I lived in Queens, I could see the Manhattan skyline and felt in awe, wowed by the sheer scale of it.

I was accepted in to the Academy of American Drama on Madison Avenue in Manhattan. Every day I had to make

The Numb and Me and Green Trainers

the hike on the L, E and 6 trains. No great shakes, I was in awe, remember? Everything was cool, nothing was a hassle. I was in love with every step of the commute. The buzz this kid from Guildford got when stepping on the train in Queens; sounds cool, edgy right? Then feeling your apprenticeship in NYC residency tested with every journey; buy a subway token, go the wrong way, another subway token, go the right way, another token, go the right way but get off the train three stops too soon. At the beginning, I was buying tokens five at a time just for good measure. Steve would help me out too if I got stuck, he thought I should get a beeper so help would be close at hand; so I did.

Walking down Madison Avenue, I looked in disbelief at every signpost. At every street corner I would marvel; wow, 24th and Madison; wow 23rd and Madison, my feet feeling electrified by the street.

I approached the stoop where a group of other young people were hanging out, eating huge slices of greasy pizza with a cigarette in the same hand. In the words of Chopper, I would need to find out 'who's who in the zoo', but not right now, everyone was a friend, everyone was cool and life was great.

When all that glitters is not gold,
And your life is not chanced to
Unfold,
With gilded dreams and ruby slippers,
Dazzled not my gems but tarmac and steam
A town of scum and jack the rippers a time must come
to bear when my learning of life is laid bare
My first oaken step from sapling darings
new limb

Housing few rings,
Nestled in the vice like grip of the ad-hoc woodsman.

It sometimes requires a sense of distance to make sense of things that are so deeply destructive and wrong.
In the moment, reality is but a sensitive cipher for your emotional, physical and spiritual self trapped or distorted by a pervasive ugliness called daily survival. If it weren't for the wafer thin link between biomechanical survival, our instinct to protect ourselves and eventually procreate, *and* our spiritual survival, a search for any hint of the sacred, we could happily ignore how dismal our chances are to wholly survive.
I would say I was an anti-survivalist; suicidal, caught between art and life, Boho in limbo, razzmatazz in a monochromatic lost city, maybe mundane in my efforts to do the same as many may have done before, maybe a desperate pioneer with a chance to open a new door in perception. Maybe I would have been a faded chalk outline of a hack novelist's fantasy or a bum note to remind the player to lick their lips before mouthing the reed, and yet I was the anti survivalist's nightmare, I lived, as social anti-matter to the enchanted people of a villainous tale.

The first people at the Academy that I met were Spike and Trent.
Spike wore his fashion identity as a true badge of intent. He was from Orange County, California and dressed like a Ska performer. He wore a strange grey Fedora hat along with yellow plaid trousers and some retro t-shirt, before all the shopping mall trendy shops

started knocking them out of their Asian 'economy' manufacturers as the next big thing.

He was broke and his wardrobe reflected this with a mish-mash of flee-market fashion but Spike pulled it off because it was true to him and subsequently carried a presence that transcended conventionality. His personality would back this up. At first meeting he was sharp tongued to the point of arrogance and spared no quarter for slack jawed dullards or mid-American moron drones. The insecurities that drove his acid cool machine would be discovered but not right away.

Trent looked scruffy, always. He was an amphetamine hippie from Vermont. He was lean to the point of being too thin other than the fact that he again pulled his look off with honesty. His drainpipe leather pants and tie dye t-shirts, fur lined jackets, buoyant curly hair, rings and chains of various design put him out to the world like a post Morrison rock star awaiting an audience, still clamoring for fuck you cool.

I was not in the midst of finding everybody fascinating in a stage-managed *joi de vivre*, I just lucked out. These two would be my faithful companions throughout my time at the Academy.

So off we went with one thing in common; we did not know what to expect inside the place we had all come some way to see.

The schedule was broken up in to core sections: Introduction to Acting; no surprise there; Voice Coaching, that seemed an overly scientific breakdown on how we make sounds from our 'instrument'; there was movement class, a class that would prove farcical as it went on; some people are just not designed to bend and twist, turn and hold graceful form; there was singing class that would have been nightmarish and cringingly embarrassing if it weren't for the fact that with two exceptions in the class, we were all rubbish; we had Alexander Technique, which coaxed us to endlessly lengthen through our spine and relax in to the cold, rigid, dusty hardwood floor; there was Comedie del l'arte, which I basically didn't like or get; Scaramouch et al unnerved me. I guess some people find out of date caricatured figures in scary masks funny or relevant in some way, I didn't.

In fact, the only highlight for me throughout this passé, pretentious, group intellectual circle jerk was when Spike accidentally engendered a passing breeze of spontaneous truth that was very funny.

Spike was jumping, leaping and all sorts of movements natural to his character. We were using a minimalist set that in real terms meant we had no set, just a few wooden cubes. Sure we could use our imagination but Spike saw to break the suspension of disbelief in a splendid way. He was mid leap from one of the boxes to another, whatever he visualized them as matters not. I suppose it was his intention to land with both feet on the other box, they didn't. He mistimed a leap and came down on a pointy corner of the box testicles first, then continued to writhe around in agonizing pain for a while. This was very amusing, far better than the script, only made better by the fact that it was our final so it was being video taped. We pinched the tape to Spike's annoyance and took it back to Trent's hovel, got high and played the episode over and over, relishing in slow-mo and reverse slow-mo the moment of impact. It was cringe making every time but delicious due to

The Numb and Me and Green Trainers

Spike's pious aggravation. The icing on the cake was Spike's 'show must go on' attitude in his approach to finishing the scene. Some may say, "How professional". I say acting, as an art form should, even in pantomime, be honest. A three feet testicle splash in my mind gives any human, actor or not, the right to say fuck this shit, my balls hurt, I'm off to find a bag of peas and a sedative.

Over the course of the year we had to study the Tragedies of the Greeks, that despite being against my principles, I enjoyed. Again, Spike was pivotal to the action and my fun. I learned a word from the TV, some car commercial that had one guy reveling in his friend's misfortune and at the end plastered the word *schadenfreuder* across the screen. I looked the word up and saw it meant one who enjoys pleasure in a friend's misfortune. Well, I know it's not that kind of me but I did enjoy ragging Spike, mainly because he was so bloody serious about the work.

We were in a scene together, two characters in Medea, who for some reason or another were really pissed off with each other. The scene required a heated argument between Spike and I. We were both dressed in homemade togas. In Spikes case this was a white bed linen folded and tied with a brown leather belt to add some authenticity. I wore a purple Terry towel, probably a hand towel, it wasn't very big. This lack of seriousness really pissed Spike off. Good, we may get some authentic emotion in the scene. Things came to a head between Spike and me, as we were awaiting our cue outside the stage. He discovered that I had taken a hit of acid before school to add an exploratory dimension to the day. He was incensed but the show must go on. So while Medea was moaning and groaning in that nauseating unreal theatrical artifice, Spike and I came barreling through the door ahead of our cue and proceeded to have a stand up brawl in front of the rest of the class and our teacher. Furious Spike, probably still smarting from my delight in showcasing his near castration, made short work of my short toga so there I was standing in some anachronistic boxers which luckily stayed on. I made head way on Spike's toga but the bugger had done a half decent job of lashing it down. Miraculously we delivered our lines through the fury. The teacher raved about Spike's performance and said mine was a little forced. Well everybody's entitled to their own opinion. I believed I was a valiant Greek somebody, said my words well and was dismissed as forced. As you can tell this stuck in my craw, so distant from the Numb, on an LSD social and *forced*. I read artificial and mediocre from forced, was I? I guess I would have to keep probing the classics to see if it was possible for a person to find universal lessons and reality from wordy, soap opera style melodrama and be unforced.

One of the most relaxing classes of the week was The History of Theatre and Film. I could latch on, albeit dispassionately, to the predictable monotonous ramblings of a sweet old codger, who, despite having an encyclopedic knowledge of film and theatre, shared none of it with us. We were given plays to read, Ibsen, Chekhov etc., I imagine, to discuss in class; this never happened. In fact nothing really ever happened. But, I somehow managed to get straight A's in the class. How? Because Mr. Jones found it vastly amusing that the pseudonym I was using at the time was the same as a notorious good guy bank robber. His slightly clouded

The Numb and Me and Green Trainers

yet sincere affection towards me was touching, though with Mr. Jones' powers of concentration as solid as mist with the attention span of a sleepy one year old, placed in tandem with my cruise control ambivalence, I was indeed lucky to get a high grade, especially as his recognition of me was only down to artifice and false perception. I doubt he could have picked me out of a line up, and he certainly never received one single piece of work from me. In a round about way Mr. Jones unwittingly pulled back the curtain in the Emerald City. He was a good man who may have lacked teaching technique but at least spared us the contrived seriousness we were having shoveled at us. He never set up machinations to deceive us, implications that there was some Mystique to what was becoming clearly an institution driven by making money and awarding super egos to a select few.

Popularity was once again at the heart of the things. Mr. Jones' class was the only part of the week that one was absent from pop politicking, unfortunately skill and hard work counted for nothing. He was stuffed in a pokey little room somewhere in the bowels of the Academy. This was suitably demeaning to this man that I wondered if various faculty members saw him as a liability; possibly because he could stumble and bumble throughout the lair and unravel the web of bullshit.

Mr. Jones' class was a musty breath of stale air that was so real, despite its inherent absurdity, it put the sanctimonious waffle about 'serious acting' and the endless popularity biased critiques about talent by failed actors in to perspective; it was all flawed.

Don't get me wrong; there were clearly systems in place to ascertain who was more competent than others. It took me back to comprehensive school in Guildford. There was an imperative in place to find the few talented heroes and weed out the rest and demote them into various stages of convenient, subservient compliance. Well, here I was again, New York City, Academy of American Drama with my green trainers on. The pack was around me and it was down to them to decide whether I had the right stuff. This time I was not prepared to stand around and await the verdict. I was to take a pre-emptive strike. At the Academy this meant doing what I wanted, not playing political games unless they proved unavoidable and generally being a brat, disrupting the status-quo ante-bellum.

I WANT TO CLARIFY SOMETHING.
I do not rant and rave about life being unfair. I do not fight to disrupt equitable meritocratic success. In fact I delight in seeing people achieve great things especially if they love what they are doing.
I do not want to present a case where I seem to negate any personal criticism, criticism of my acting, dancing, singing et al. I am not so deeply seated in insecurity that any negative critique I receive, I arbitrarily write off to avoid a total collapse in my weathered self-esteem. I don't care if somebody says I'm shit at something. I don't even care if somebody who inspires awe and respect challenges my qualities and failures and surmises I'm a little rough around the edges or incomplete technically or a little green. I want to avoid at all costs being half-assed and lazy when it comes to art.
I feel it important to make the distinction between being evaluated on your talent and promise, requiring a rather occult and obscure calculator and evaluation

of talent and promise determined by how much your peers, teachers and administrative staff want to touch you, rub against you like a cat feigning affection, truly laying a territorial scent *and* how your affable personality and Mr. Nice Guy attitude make people trust in your consistent wonderfulness, charm and greasy-slick, sycophantic, yes man half man routine.

In some cases there were examples of meritocracy working free from social influence. In dance class I was shit. My teacher was lovely and I was pleasant to her but that was that. Singing class was a similar story. I was marginally better at singing than dance and the Broadway obsessed teacher at the piano was fair. Could you sing the notes on the page? Yes, good, no, bad. Sure you could kiss his ass and flatter his ego a little and squeeze a fraction of a grade out of him but once again that was all there was to that.

My beef was with the acting teachers. They were in my mind the artistic equivalent of fast food restaurant managers, ensuring carbon copy excellence was kept on the production line of indifferent mediocrity, with a mandate issued from the top: take the money and smile; next?

They were the mob around the boy with green trainers. Their opinion of you personally almost certainly influenced their decisions of you as an artist. Remove any fawning and ass licking and you were done for.

And there was the rub. I wasn't particularly likeable, made little effort to be sweet to the blah-Muppet acting teachers and subsequently felt that any critique of me as an artist was poisoned by their brittle, damaged egos. I know some people are born to teach and that is certainly a good thing but in the acting world you'd be hard pressed to find an individual who was teaching as a first choice. Yep, they were us, just a couple of generations removed from the hope of stardom. But they were only human.

Well, newsflash, this was art; meant to be fucking cutting edge stuff pushing at the boundaries of what existed and moving forward with the assistance of new blood and ideas. I know I was awkward which made me a misfit at the Academy, but being nice surely wasn't requisite. My confrontational attitude should not have marginalized me and labeled me mediocre. My veins coursed with passion, I lived and breathed art, not in a superficial toadying way, and wanted to push acting further towards truth. Being popular was not on my list of priorities.

I was starting to think the Academy and I were not very good bedfellows; I know they agreed.

I saw the Academy as a grey machine with all the same tedious social dimensions that should have stopped at their front door. This dusty institution turned out to be a quirk of fate, a ruse concocted between the Numb and the deep blue sea to have me positioned in New York. My desire to be part of the action on a bigger scale than was being offered was immense. This desire was not fuelled by social niceties; if I wanted nice I could have sucked up more, but that was not my path. The Academy invited the most promising talent back for the second year, and then maybe a place in the hallowed 'company' that comprised of a nurtured bunch of sycophants who may well have been talented artists but

The Numb and Me and Green Trainers

equally may have just been talented politicians. Either way I was not invited back.

I did, over the course of the year, have a social life that was passionate. This took me on an unguided trip around the underbelly of Manhattan and was almost certainly responsible for my failures at the Academy.

✭ ✭ ✭

I wanted to immerse myself in Big City culture. The problem was I was still living in Queens; once a place of tantalizing dreams of the city, now a barrier between the Numb's imperative: fitting in on my own terms.

Before moving to a city, without prior knowledge of what to expect, you are largely flexible about all sorts of things that eventually become suffocating or excruciatingly difficult to accept. I felt my race had been run in Queens. It was obvious that the one hour plus daily commute each way would get tedious once I got used to it. There were two forces at work here that made things complicated.

The first issue was what I called 'the Film Set Mirage'. The trip in to the city always held promise of something exciting. It felt that you were going the right direction. The return trip was like an expose' of the two dimensionality of the façade. There was nothing wrong with Queens at all, but with the Manhattanites filling the roles: the producers, the director and the stars in the fantasy, the Queens bound journey felt like a view at the blank side of the Technicolor; the carpenters joining one piece of wood to another, the electricians rigging up the lights for the big show on the other side.

So that was problem Number one. Problem Number two, and I know how hypocritical this sounds, was that a part of me loved coming back to Queens especially when Steve would pick me up from the station and spare me the excitement killing, twenty minute walk back into the too quiet residential neighborhoods. The veneration and disappointment in Steve would become apparent but these moments spent with him in the well-used and plush armchair like seats of his Cadillac felt like an education in the darker side of life. Steve taught me two things.

The first thing Steve taught me was how to make a drink called a 'Machine'. He, with his large hands, would with surgical precision float just the right amount of orange juice on top of two ounces of cheap vodka into a shot glass. This created a drink, if you could call it that with a straight face that was devastating to the head department and quite refreshingly orangey on the palette. So there it was, the Machine, a learned life skill that I could dazzle peasant children and world leaders alike.

The second wonderment that Steve introduced me to would change my life forever.

Steve and some of his friends were off to see an American Football game, Dallas Cowboys against the New York Giants. I was asked to go along. This was massively exciting for me. My first ever game, with the man who had taught me the Machine, how could I refuse.

So we got to the game; Steve drove, met his friends there, was slipped a Milwaukee Best, known to the natives as The Beast; no time for fancy mixology here just cheap beer, and for me this was great.

The Numb and Me and Green Trainers

"Can I get another one?"
"Shit kid, you finished that already? See that guys, I told you about the kid". There were a few chuckles and then it happened. Steve gave me a small piece of folded magazine paper about the size of a stick of gum. I looked down perplexed, despite my exposure to endless quantities of weed, booze, ecstasy, a little special k and angel dust I was remarkably naïve about the whole process of buying drugs and their respective paraphernalia.

If this sounds implausible to you then go out and do all of this yourself. If your way differs then great, you've delved deep in to the underbelly of life and for what, to prove me wrong. Trust me on this; I was naïve to the mechanics of drug wrappings, dealings and utensils because I wanted to be, the Numbs protection of my innocence.

It is very hard to be led blindly in to a trap, down a slippery slope or any other euphemism for a subterranean lifestyle choice. You usually have two eyes open and there are few if any 'bad influences' out there that have anything to gain by deliberately sabotaging another person's life. Lonely people attract lonely people in the same way as most other social groups. In any social groups there are individuals with dominant or submissive tendencies, however slight or opaque, that once slotted in to place form the compass for the group. You lead yourself and sometimes things turn out shitty and it's hard to reconcile yourself to yourself; mind, body and soul; and the decisions you made. But that doesn't make you blind. If anything you have your eyes open wider than those who drift by on the slow river of indifference. Your senses are alive and tingling and you choose to bridge social boundaries, bounding across a bridge that is already smoldering and burning your feet without a second of concern about coming back.

I chose that day, eyes wide open, to go in to the unknown.

That day was exciting. I had just been given a small piece of magazine paper and was about to open it right there and then in the stadium car park. I had rarely seen such a collective groan from a group of grown men, in this case Steve's friends, as I was about to let what I would later know to be a gram of Cocaine scatter into muddy ground around the portaloo we had all migrated around.

So I stood there in my green trainers desperate for someone to give me instructions. Holy shit, once more I was faced with a dilemma, was I mediocre again? Only in this case was I actually bad at taking drugs? I had surmised that there must have been something drug-like in the wrapper after the group gasp and was nodded towards the porta-cabin. It was my time,

"Hey Kid d' ya have a bill",

Oh shit. Had I presumed this was a gift? Had I unwittingly entered in to a non-verbal agreement concerning the sale of these drugs to me, had I trampled upon recognized social taboo?

The Numb intervened,

"Yeh",

And I proceeded to the luxury of the blue mini-shed with piss stained floors; in fact piss stained everything, I stood in the middle, not wanting to touch the sheen of urine that coated everything, and there was the

The Numb and Me and Green Trainers

smell; not quite shit but only because some chemical so strong was degrading some other persons turd with such power that the turd, which is quite an adversary in the stench department, was defeated hands down.

So in this setting I fumbled open the magazine paper desperately trying not to drop it in to the utter nastiness that lurked under the sticky, broken-hinged, pissed stained seat. In fact any wobble or spasm of the hand would have rendered my first cocaine moment a big nothing, followed by crap lies about how I felt high all day but, to my credit I got the paper open and saw what looked like any other white powder. With familiarity comes expertise, an eye of experience, the ability to differentiate one white powder from another; appreciating nuance in texture and the shading. I had spent no time in my life examining or even paying attention to the white powders I had come in to contact with; washing powder, sugar, salt, you get my point.

The first thing I did was wet my finger and have a little dab in to the powder and put it to my tongue. The sensation was bizarre. I hadn't known people before who openly talked about doing cocaine so I had no first hand knowledge of what the experience would be like. My tongue tingled and fizzled, not like those popping candies you get as a kid, in a more internal sense of tingling, but that was it. All those cop films, where they have a dab, look to their partner and give a knowing nod was all I knew as reaction to what I had just done. This was as good a reference point as I had. My tongue was numb, proof positive that the powder was not baking powder, and as I had no partner to bounce off, I looked down at the blue-grey slurry in the diabolical toilet hole and nodded knowingly. The powder was collected mainly in the crease of the paper. I crouched down and placed the open wrap of paper on my shoe then took the dollar bill, thanks Numb for not making me look like a twat earlier, rolled it up with my hand slightly quivering by this time and realized the moment had arrived. I picked the wrap up in my left hand and held the bill in the other, raising it to my right nostril, probing the powder like a blind man's cane searching for a curb, then sniffed really hard. Without covering my left nostril my suction power was lacking but I managed to force at least some of the coke up my nose and in to my brain.

All of a sudden I got really anxious about the time I had been in this stinking cabin and dreaded going out to face ridicule from strangers. I folded the wrap back up and with a nod put the stuff in to my pocket, wiped at my nostrils and then opened the door. It must have been paranoia creeping in because no one made any reference to my time away. Steve asked the inevitable question, I said 'good', with an over rehearsed nod of my head. He patted me on the shoulder and took his turn in the blue room, as I shall now call it to create a sense of ambiguous pleasantness, came out again in what seemed like seconds and said," Let's go see the Giants kick those pussy Cowboys asses". A last chug of my beer and then we were off to the seats. After about five minutes the beer caught up with me and I needed to piss; I told the guys, they responded, "Oh yeh. Go on then, but it's gotta last ya all day". What? I really needed to go; I wasn't craving another bit of coke, although it did sit restlessly in my pocket. So off I went, took a leak and while I was there my hand crept in to my pocket. What the hell, I didn't understand the game upstairs, kept starting and stopping for no apparent reason, or the game here in the toilets, but I knew which one grabbed my interest. Fuck it. Excess started here and now. I found a ledge of sorts in the toilet cubicle, unpacked my drugs, got my dollar bill out; already like a seasoned pro, put my finger over my left nostril and sucked until all the powder had been vacuumed in to my head. I felt a rush to my head like a dormant part of my brain had just been awoken in a Frankensteinian moment.

The Numb was yelling "I'm alive, I'm alive I tell you", cackling wildly at the polarity of the situation. I had just got higher than ever before in my life whilst descending in one shot to the insanity of addiction.

High, I was, Low I would be. Really, really high and really fucking low.

But this, Queens, was my dress rehearsal in preparation for the main event across the east river. All coked up and nowhere to go except the wonderful fabulous, glorious shiny, shimmering kaleidoscope wonder called the Me Destruction show.

Back to that Giant's stadium toilet, now paranoid again about time and my perceived mismanagement of it, I'd been gone too long, had anyone heard the goings-on inside my box, had anyone sensed . . .

No, I was free and clear except for being treetop high. Dollar bill went back in pocket, I licked the magazine paper; it was the first time I had ever licked magazine paper, before crumpling it up and throwing down the toilet. Endless paranoid delusions filled my mind about how this paper was going to gum up the whole works and I would be left standing, no levitating, having to explain the whole mess. The paper went down without a pause for thought; another crisis solved, what was I doing again? Oh yeh, Giants and Cowboys shooting it out Western style and today I wasn't going to miss the tin cans, but tomorrow I would want more, more machines, more coke. I knew a lot of tomorrows had passed by the time my stash smelled synonymous with its hiding place, behind a bottle of Calvin Klein Be.

Steve was a great party buddy, and I hope now you can see why I loved coming back to Queens, but it really was time for something to happen to force my hand in to the City.

That something was a 5ft 5-inch sex machine, beautiful and alluring with a southern drawl, a lap dancer's body and huge brown eyes. On top of this she was semi-famous; she'd been the head piece of sexual merchandising for a music video whose one hit wonder band achieved a one hit, Number one. The song was given hours of airtime the summer before I met Sophie. She turned heads, she would have done anyway, but with the saturation coverage of the MTV video, she was pushed into her fifteen minutes of fame.

The first time I saw her, I didn't recognize her for being this sexpot quasi-starlet. I saw a hot, super sexy, pneumatic fuck machine with saucepan eyes, full lips, pert breasts and a bum, well, lets just say where I came from we 'aint seen bums like those before.

The pizza shop next to the Academy had a pool table; I momentarily stopped outside to the front of the Academy, to hear that six months had passed and a new intake of girls were due to arrive and one of them had already been in this music video. I didn't know where she was in the city but my feet guided me down the steps of the pizza shop, and with simplicity, as in seeing an illusion and accepting it as fact, we immediately were attracted to each other, she became the partner to my illusionary double act.

There was some tension but more excitement; what was going to happen, how was I going to land the deal, was I going to fuck things up?

Other girls sneered at her as she walked passed, huddled together discussing how inappropriate her clothes were for the Academy.

Sophie walked up to me at the end of daily class and asked if I wanted to go up and hang out at her place.

So I went to hang out, a few hours later we were naked, a few seconds later we were going at it like two animals who truly wanted to devour each other.

I wanted to writhe and interlock with her like two demons cast down, lustful and complete, I loved worshipping her body. We had this energy from day one. We would soon be living together and I was in Manhattan; she had what she wanted and I had my perfect trophy girl who ignited my loins and added to my conspiracy against mediocrity.

Steve, oh Steve, what a gift you had given me. I did not exclusively blame him for the cocaine, getting me started, which could have happened at any time, but it didn't happen anytime, it happened then, and I now had a desire to find coke wherever I could. Lucky for me a card was put in my hand one day by somebody I can't recall. The card had 666 on it and a beeper number.

In New York City there were so many delivery services for weed. These couriers occasionally carried other bits and pieces. There was something ominous about the card with 666 on it and the face of a playing card.

I was always aware of Satan and Hell for as long as I could remember. I guess I went to the right churches. I was never turned on to organized religion, but as is so fashionable to say these days, I see myself as a person who operates morally within my own perimeters, some of the time.

So what does that make me, a hypocrite? No not really, I like to feel the human process is one of increasing learning: to change gears, change perceptions or avoid continuity. This may attract outside influences calling you all sorts of names, heathen, Satanist, addict, well I'm not much for "ists" or "isms".
I guess at this point in my life if I had to, I would classify myself as a cheerless activist for humanitarianism.
Vast swathes of my time were spent in introspective self-flagellation, but in an effort to keep track, I would say that seeing 666, then a beeper number on a card was designed to be, and was, a little unnerving.
So one day I called the 666 and left a number to call me back. I guessed if it was Satan himself he would probably not need to waste time with beepers, pager numbers and cell phones, so as bad as this person was, I think I overcame the first line of his defenses: keep out all who do not wish to have their pure Christian hearts devoured by me, Satan. So there I was in limbo, waiting for the call.
When it came I picked up.
"You call me?"
"Yes I got given one of your cards."
"Oh, well where d'you live?"

Oh shit here we go. I was about to give my name and address to somebody whose only marketing was cribbed from the Devil.

"Oh, it's 100th street between Broadway and Amsterdam."

"Okay, see you later".

Had the deal with the devil been done or was this standard practice amongst your higher end coke dealing gangs?

Had I let the cat out the bag big time? I got anxious, had I done the right thing?

Then, before I knew it my phone rang.

"Yo, what's up, it's me."

"Okay I'll buzz you up".

I frantically looked around the four hundred square foot apartment wondering if there was any thing I could do to make the place look nice. Then I thought about protecting myself, looked at a kitchen knife, and dismissed that right off. Whatever I started would not end with a blunt kitchen knife, so I put the kettle on and lit a cigarette.

Knock knock. Here we go.

I wilted as this huge guy dressed to the nines in cool looking expensive gangsta gear stood massive in the doorway; it was only when he came in mine and Sophie's tiny apartment that I saw he had brought another slightly smaller version of himself along for the ride.

A blunt kitchen knife, yeah, maybe in a Jackie Chan movie. But that wasn't the vibe. It was quite tense, but not aggressive, just a new experience in weird. I broke the ice by offering them a cup of tea, it was at this point that one of the guys in what sounded like an effeminate New York and Royal Family-ish accent said to his friend, "yeah, do you want some tea and crumpets?" I thought I was about to face a beating for being a queer, crumpet eating Englishman, when the guy said it again, the first guy laughed and the guy who did the imitation said, "yo, that shit is so cool."

I said, "thanks", half smiling, "but do you want-".

"No thanks man, but that's cool".

Then the bigger one saw a headshot of Sophie above the fridge and said,

"You, you know this girl?"

I said, "Yes she's my girlfriend"

"No shit, really? No shit. Are you for real, oh well kid you must have got sumthin."

With that the ice was broken, maybe for a first meeting things had gone well, but it was still time for business.

I showed him eighty dollars and asked what I could get with it. He glanced to his friend then took more coke than I'd ever seen before, and said, "How's this?"

"Great!"

He then smiled, told me his name, his buddy told me his and they were gone; it was all surreal, except for the large bag of coke on the kitchenette table.

Well I say a large bag, by the standards of what was to come this was a mere fraction, but the bag of powder was mine. In the process of my drug use, as I had mentioned before, I was usually a passive recipient of other people's efforts in the set-up. In this case it was all me. And it was alarmingly pedestrian in tone, like an everyday thing. But this was far from an everyday thing for me; this was another giant leap forward in my involvement with the forbidden.

I think there is a clear distinction between the passive, occasionals in drug use and the regulars, psychologically speaking that is. The premeditation, my page to 666, and the end result, my own bag of drugs, was executed well and tore down barriers of emotional resistance anyone, or should I say most people would have in this environment.

My conclusion; I had come a long way from small wraps of powder donated by Steve at the ball game and had become a qualified purchaser of class A drugs.

The normalcy of what went down was the nightmare. The absence of shadowy figures, meeting in dark alleys, getting ripped off, killed or worse in the murky, occult world I had imagined. The delivery was like ordering a pizza with one exception, the efficiency and unproblematic nature of the supply and demand chain, and at the end of the day you were getting something lovingly handled prior to delivery, no half-folded over pie with anchovies instead of pepperoni, the right goods on time. Great, I guess the question remained though, how did I know this bag of powder was good, was I a gullible mug who just got stung? I had little experiential knowledge to decipher what was good and what was not. Well I had one way to sort this out and as you know the proof of the pudding is in the eating, so with no further ado, dinnertime.

As an obsessively selfish person, I always had issues with the seemingly meager rations such magical powder was given out. When other people had put in the spadework you engendered a deferential role in order to get portioned out your scraps, smile and wait for the conductor's next nod to you for another blow up the meat trumpet.

The other way of doing things was being a "fiend", as we described them. These were those hangers-on in your group who you felt little for, but as a court jester entertains, everybody needs a fool in the social scene to create a sense of superiority for those who were the holders of the holy bag: the selected, political few, who got loads of extra lines, and the patient ones who took their medicine well. Holy shit, what a sub-culture mind-fuck this all was. Here is the most base dealing with base, the most funnel nosed debased were only a political flick from the subsection; fiend, by the party elite.

See Numb, nothing to worry about, social dysfunction and politics were rife, and it was up to us to find out what we wanted, how political we wanted to be and how entrenched in this sub-culture we could get while keeping an eye on the big picture, keep real, stay focused. I knew this was going to degenerate sub dermis as fast as I would shine and sparkle in the stratosphere of self-made attention laden captains of drug culture party management.

What a headache, how about doing something I never did before.

I took out a bank card, poured an amount of the coke on the table, the stuff that wasn't all bunched up, I poured out a little more, cut the chalky white powder in to one line about six inches long, poured a shot of Jack Daniels, don't know why, this proved a distraction. Which one first, shot or line, then bang. Like a man on a mission I took a bill out of my pocket, happened to be a twenty, hey going up in the world, this made me smile, rolled it, not too tight then descended over the cornrow I put out for myself and with a huff and a puff,

The Numb and Me and Green Trainers

Straight to my brain, do not pass go; do not collect $200. The dizzying pitter-patter of snowflakes softly tingling my scalp, my head felt cold and awake. I reeled on my heels then grinned, a Cheshire cat grin, a love of life that required drinking and smoking to join the party immediately.

Clever boy with the shot, it went down without touching the sides, should I have another, sure why not, I was pouring it, now anxious as to where Mr. Cigarette had gone off to, everything was going so well. I popped the next shot, but this was getting too much, needed to smoke, scared of going outside the door to the store, now here it's a bodega, the porno pushing bodega boss was large in character, all I wanted were smokes, it was just around the block, but what a block, was it safe to leave my stash, was it fair to leave, okay, gotta go. Picked up the bag, took a dab just for good measure, wow, Numb, there you go, the booze was good but one side of a coin I needed to toss before round two would start, bag away, checked nose in mirror, no white, good, put on a big coat, found a five dollar bill scrunched up this was good, going out was going to be bad, but to the bodega onwards.

I hustled down the stairs, I was lucky in that nobody in the building talked to me anyway, then the street, turned left at the stoop to Broadway, turned a corner and voila the bodega of booze, cigarettes, dildos and knives, bongs and one hitter, porn, and then some special porn he kept for his favorite customers.

I went to the man, "camel lights, and some matches", "oh I have Houston 500, and she bangs 500 men. Man, how about that", "no thanks just camels and matches". I rifled through my pocket, couldn't find the five, where did I put it, oh there it was in my left hand, oh well I guess this was my first lesson in discerning good drugs from bad in my friendly convenience store, "oh and cinnamon gun, I mean gum, the one that fizzes", "yeh, I know the stuff guy", a sizzle, bubble on tongue to magnify the sweet delicious brain fry.

So gum, cigarettes and matches, no orgy porn today I had other things on my mind. Like a secret agent I ghosted my way back to the grotto. But things were different, where had the party gone, oh I remembered, I had desperately wanted to smoke not so much now, bang there it is. The party needed a kick-start again, my absenteeism had sent the engine stalling, free falling back to sobriety with nasty booze breath to boot. Damn auto pilot, not to be trusted. I got the bag, chose a line of coke, poured my drink, cigarette ready,

3-2-1-lift-off.

As they say on the back of shampoo bottles repeat if needed. Well okay, see you on the cold slope of desolation; I'll be there on cue, oblivious, self-obsessive denial, but no Numb! Not now. We're having ourselves a party.

When you're a control freak as I most certainly am, a well stocked party of one can outshine many a majestic ball or a deliciously Bacchanalian dinner with a host of shallow shallot ragu munchers, amused with the amuse`, never a disappointment to mange tout, never to ferme le bouche. Waiting in line to enter a claustrophobic dungeon-like nightclub, well if you are a true kinky devil, let the music be the food of lust and play on. But I'm not talking about the pre-planned dungeon life, I'm talking about the negligently proportioned, wine cellar-esque shit holes, despite the prohibitively

offensive, yet honestly meritocratic, albeit in a superficial way, door policy, the getting in was better than being in. The prices of the drinks were outrageous. Of the many awful squalid pits of exhaustion around Manhattan The Cave was probably the worst.
So I was not a huge fan of going out, way too many variables out of control plus the inevitable inclusion of your friends and acquaintances, who would be all over your drugs like a rash, your only hope was that you could be all over theirs.
So my party was fun, no sharing, no caring, just selfish oblivion. Time was suspended in the silent methodology between drugs, cigarettes and Jack Daniels. Nobody was calling or paging which kind of irked me. It was wonderful to be here with my selfish stage-managed solo-bop, but with nobody to lord it all over, the scene was lacking.
The friends, we'll call them that so I can spare you endless tedium of the distinction between friends, acquaintances, fiends or hangers on or newbie's right off the bus from somewhere else; let's just call them all friends because there is a commonality between all of them: they were all short changed and spiteful because I was emotionally bankrupt. Sure I had endless emotions pouring out of my pores, drug, especially ecstasy, induced deep and meaningfuls with my friends, but I truly invested nothing in them. There were deep usury undertones with our entire group. It was just a matter of who's gonna use who tonight. There was no tomorrow, not just in a fake rock and roll existentialist contrivance, but because it had to be squeezed out to allow the life of the moment to breath deeply. Most of the gatherings were surrounded around the subtle

engineering of scoring as many free drugs as possible from your friends without your stash being plundered. It was a war of attrition in which a variety of tricks and scheming would be learned in order to be victorious in this war craft more often than not.

This system allowed the occasional fiend in, just for entertainment, who was usually the most misery member of the group. This person would have the same ideas of taking drugs as the rest, but a difference in opinion to the rest about how to budget properly, a lofty superior attitude preaching the virtues of using money shrewdly, beyond the party life. These were all things we didn't want to hear, we drug addled actors. It was demeaning to our world to be marginalized by Spike who would regularly imply that some people, meaning him, were not as fortunate as others and had other responsibilities than chipping in on a bag of drugs he would happily quaff on anyone else's ticket.

There was an inherent superiority being the one in the group holding the bag. This person was centre of attention and would control the Pavlovian pack awaiting their signal. This was quite a task and in order to ensure having things run smoothly an ally was needed. It was crucial that a sub-contracted official, who had to be well liked in the group, helped maintain order; the pay-off, well what do you think?

It was considered an unspoken law that you could all use each other. What was unacceptable was to use someone and then develop a conscience about it. This guilt could be a real fly in the ointment, a speck of grit in the eyes of you and your friends. With guilt came defensiveness, with that there was conflict and this was incredibly disruptive to the group. The bubble was quite resilient but it couldn't withstand a saboteur intent on bursting it.

So drug culture parties were not honest, the talk was fake, though you may have discovered a nugget of truth in the process of talking about a topic ad nauseam. But who wanted to pick through the corn, peas and bile to pick up the sliver of humanity that may have been coughed up. Drug culture parties were, as the Numb and I discovered, completely out of whack with convention and the ordinary functions of life, yet still were bound by traditional disingenuous terrestrial politicking, maintaining trust and acts of generosity in the hope of later remembrances and reciprocity.

The nuts and bolts of it were alarmingly Langley-esque in many ways: cold, callous, narcissistic and self-involved. I should have paid more attention then, maybe. Or maybe I should have taken stock and seen what a short journey I had actually made.

That's why the blissfully ignorant beauty of this moment must be revered. I was in complete control. I could kick start this whole lurid chain of political events in to action, knowing that in spite of my early start in the party, if and impromptu gathering was sprung, I would be top dog. Was it worth giving up the serenity and control for an ego inflating taste of friendship; impure and phony, a visceral anchor to life, a need to feed drugs to my friends so that I could vampirically feed from their life force.

What a super cynical way of looking at things, I know. But unfortunately in the day-to-day world of addiction, call it early days of, severe or anything else, came an overwhelming sense of selfish control of what was yours. Some friends feigned largesse and philanthropy but it all boiled down to control, and unfortunately control mostly came from cash flow, but also one's chosen level of involvement in the drug pit.

With all this introspection I forgot all about the one person at this stage that I was falling in love with. Sure the dice were loaded, and this one was going to have some small wins but crap out eventually, but it was only a matter of time.

But, back to the moment: Sophie, the goddess. The Numb had allowed me to have her exempt from the dirty festering wound my coke addiction had become, from the uncared for scratch from Steve's poisoned thorn, a rot had set in, worsened, and I didn't want Sophie to be a part of the disease.

Seeing Abby's billowing hair just for a moment then, back to life. Sophie was no Abby, but did I need an Abby in my life, a pure kind heart to nurse me back to hope, or was this an illusion, a taunt from the Numb of things passed and gone. If I needed Sophie to be Abby I was in deep trouble, but just maybe there was some room to trust life, and trust Sophie, on a heart level.

So in a matter of seconds, minutes, hours, I had no clock to tock and tick with my ticks of anxiety and tocks of mockery.

I had valued, dismissed, reassessed, cogitated and realized I was standing up in the same spot in the kitchen, cigarette in hand, cigarette being stubbed out carelessly in a semi crowded ash tray. I fancied a drink, but the liquor seemed fierce now, unless I had a chaser to drive things on.

What to do,

Know clue,

Got drugs,

The Numb and Me and Green Trainers

Not good at being in control of the bag,
Got smokes,
Half a pack,
Had I been careless with the sack of white,
Need some hydration,
Anything no alcho was considered,
Without a doubt, pointless,
But what about tea,
Sounds good,
But what about the bubbles,
No bubble in tea, so beer for me,
To the bodega,
Easier this time, not so hung up with that initial freeze of paranoia, been there once, came back once, today, odds were on my side.
But what if,
There were others,
Not bodegas,
Although I'm sure there are thousands, my thoughts bend to the friends, of which there were not,
But only one needed to bring beer, to keep things moving forward.
What about Sophie, when was she home, what was she up to, she could bring beer, no politics, just us in a cocoon of genetic flaw, beautiful butterflies, too dumb to fly, but safe in the knowledge of beauty, not I, tortured by the vacuous emptiness in my thoughts and reconciliations to past moral jeopardy, cocoon to cuckold, cuckold to cocoon.
Self made traps are no less deadly and purposeful in action, mice don't make good vermin trap makers, they like the cheese too much for their own good, my trap, my iron maiden cocoon was ill devised cause I too liked

my cheese, beauty fettered with the nectar mine to own, no extra cocoon fluttering of eyelids or wings, or poison arrow pierce my heart, and leave me Numb.

The writing was on the wall, my friends were shit and my girlfriend was no Abby-esque angel, I just still had a bunch to learn about life, and the Numb let the strife and pain come thick and fast without refrain.
So who to call, Spike, no can't handle the bullshit, Trent, maybe, oh hell why not, "Trent will ya bring beer?" Pause. "No not that good flavored Sierra Nevada, something light and cold."
"Sure, we having a party?"
"Come on up and have a look see, oh and bring some smokes."
"Already got them."

So there it was done, the wheels were in motion, spare the fact Trent nearly always was a more than equal sharer in the game, we had loads and could rock star it up. Trent and I were cracking some beers, so,
SO?
Oh you mean this, I unfurled the bag of coke and Trent's eyes twinkled with delight and madness. He knew the drill, I led off as master of ceremonies, cut two oversize lines to show off mainly and we took to the starting line and away, stood up, eyes rolling then high fived each other,
"Hey thanks man."
"No need", the politics were working as per usual, beer guzzled down my neck, then Jack Daniels, more high fives, cigarette time as we embarked upon the inevitable talk of the dead. In that I mean the mutual admiration

society, for and beyond normal social etiquette, "yeah, your song the other day in Morris' class, yeah, kicked ass", as a huge plume of smoke emptied his mouth and nostrils.
Really I loved to be flattered on vocal cause I knew I was not good, coupled with the fact Trent had the worst voice in the class, always sang really bad songs, the compliment sunk in the epidermis where it jostled my fingers towards another cigarette.
Actors who are high talking about acting is not very interesting but to surmise,
"You were great in that scene."
"Mr. X was a real asshole to you regarding . . ."
"I thought you nailed it, go on, and sing, just a little . . ."
All heavy smoking and coke stained mirrors.

So off we went, having a right old time of it then kerclunk, twist, squeak, who could that be at the door, I know, the only other person with a key, Sophie.
Sophie was late, not that I particularly noticed, but apparently despite being in the throws of partying the Numb could give me moments of clarity. Sophie was back late, I had noticed, no point being nonchalant, and I was caught between my poison cocoon and my superficial superstar synopsis.

I will continue being true to the moment, with omniscience it is all so clear, but back then, I felt pissed Sophie was back later than usual, dealt with it passive aggressive style, not wanting to seem a caveman, oblivious of course to how she must have felt coming

home maybe for a very good reason late, seeing Trent and I turn our miniscule hovel in to a drug den.
As fortune favors the brave, maybe it also savors the depraved. Sophie, without a pause for thought, without taking her coat off, looking so sexy, couldn't show that feeling in front of Trent, not noticing Trent noticing her looking very sexy not wanting me to see, cause that would have started shit, Sophie seeing all says,
"Count me in boys".

And there it was, except for a Trent bodega run for essentials we partied till all was gone, except that little bag that was just for ones private moments, time to wrap things up, well no not exactly.
Trent poured a shot of Jim Beam now, couldn't tell the difference, sat us down, as if to break some headline news, reached in to his bag and pulled out the black container designed to hold film. But as he opened the lid, lifted the shot glasses high, poured out the contents of some white powder and said, "cheers", with a beaming, lottery win smile his ace in the hole, his challenge to me, would he go the whole way, he did reward my stash. But deep in one of those pockets squirreled away for the cold dawn of coming down, a vulgar wrenching experience, best suffered alone, Trent had another small pouch, but so did I, we had played a good game, so time to drink; the bourbon was like grit in my throat, must have been the cigarettes, or maybe it was the special cigarettes.
You see we cut some more lines, had a snort but after a while your nostrils gum up. You can't suck anything up there; usually after a heavy session as that night had been, both nostrils were gummed up, and with

The Numb and Me and Green Trainers

super-vac broke, and the party needing progression we had to improvise.

See in the excess, excess becomes normalcy. It would occur to most people, even those who were un-censorious concerning drug use, if you had gummed one, let alone two nostrils up with large quantities of coke, it was probably time to call it a day. But in the mode of excess, those who have been part of the party from early on usually want to continue to the bitter end, or as I said earlier to that time when like a wounded animal the time comes to take off to lick your wounds, or like an ignoble Cossack, tired after a raid, taking to the safety of the mountains to re-coup to fight another day.

So the march onwards . . .
With two blocked nostrils and cocaine to be taken, what was one to do? Dabbing on the gums was a fun perk at the intro stages of the party, but not for now. We got the idea to dip the end of our cigarettes about one centimeter in bourbon then roll the moist end in the coke. This cigarette would be left to dry, then BOOM! Freebasing,
Headaches, paranoia, disorientation, but beer now, bourbon too harsh, a couple more regular smokes, then another special cigarette, Trent and I agreed we didn't like this, too harsh, buzz kill,
But over the course of our party lives we would forget that true grim reaper presence that freebasing brought on time and time again.
These special cigarettes had pretty much done for me. I went to lay down, too much of a good thing. As for Trent and Sophie, who knew? At that point I was burnt out, not even the Numb could save me here.

Euan Sutton

No touch, just rubbery contact,
Digits melt into spade hand, couldn't
Dig a raw nerve though, no go,
no libido, sexless, below the waist
mechanical failure, in the dome, operational
failure.
Burn out, not Numb, no, not Numb
I could feel,
That feeling was dying.

Emptiness with bodies next door,
No life left to explore,
The body shutting down
Without the strength to
Long for home,
Burn out, not Numb, not Numb
I would feel
Alone.

Next day: re-birth or afterbirth?
The day after a heavy amphetamine night is rarely a happy productive one. You wake up in a state of almost total disorientation. Often dehydrated and ill rested, it is hard to make sense of what came before and subsequently leaves a shaky foundation of what is to follow.
So I had become a party addict. I purposefully use the word "party", not as a euphemism for drug addict. I am not attempting to play down the pivotal role, taking and eventually becoming addicted to drugs, had in the overall picture of party addict. I had become hooked on the whole process, politics and undeniable chaos that surrounded the scene.
With this in mind it is hard to imagine how one could control other normal factors in life. I mean I had a girlfriend, who I lived with, the conclusion of the relationships will be arrived at later, but how could I have been a good boyfriend? I was enrolled full time at the Academy of American Drama. How could I, even with talent, achieve much if anything when continually living to maneuver myself ever towards the center of the party culture? Well, as I said before, Sophie was no angel, but with my motivations as they were, I was completely blind to exactly how bad things were between us. As the summer of her fifteen-minute fame turned to autumn of forgotten then winter of cold obscurity, how much had she changed? Her desires, insecurities and motivation must have ebbed and flowed, but even living in such close proximity to her, I noticed very little. I did notice that she had an entirely new set of just her friends, mostly male, that upon arriving home, I would see cutting up lines of various drugs for her. As long as

there was a line cut out for me and common courtesy from her friends, I took nothing in.

Things had become grey and lifeless between us, not that I noticed at the time. We shared very little, and she developed an antagonistic streak towards my drug use. Yeah, she was embroiled in a similar thing, but now with different people, a different crowd and therefore different politics, rules and sensibilities. I was the belligerent fiend in their circle whilst maintaining, as I thought, firm political control of my position in mine, so when that cold day after hits the reset button of consciousness, had I somehow slipped, become passé, or had I just become too boring to be around. Was Sophie's pointed judgment a mirror image to what was happening in my crowd? I had partied hard with Spike, Trent, and Rex for some months, but I had become a new breed. I had evolved, genetically mutated in to a new type of drugs fiend; a super fiend, monstrous and bullish in attempts to sate selfish desires. I had let all common rules of decency and social values collapse under the force of my experimentation. Or maybe I had just become too vulgar and unpleasant to be around. Spike's resentment towards the party scene or should I say my designs for our group dynamic, had actually stirred him to partially remove himself from taking drugs, and concentrate more on his acting. He was talented and had the group (and again when I say group it is more an attempt to drag others kicking and screaming into the fray, I really mean just me, selfish and alone) been more ready to accept humility, Spike's revised attitude may have been good for all of us; at the time his cold shoulder felt like betrayal. As an addict, I was in denial and was myopic and selfish; when somebody started

The Numb and Me and Green Trainers

challenging my completely irrational choices, choices torturously slow moving and non-sequitur due to the "reset sensation" post mortem, it was unlivable with to have somebody approach me on logic or reason driven premises; they're not asked for, not wanted and just too painful to bear. Spike pushed on with his agenda, showing clearly if I had had the eyes to see, the bubble had already burst, and I was holding on to a false present, a party anachronism. Rex, a guy not mentioned too much, due to the nature of the negativity I brought to him; he had a wonderful singing voice, and during our parties was often urged to entertain us. Our group allowed change to happen to Rex. I feel so responsible for the way a shy, humble talent like Rex's, morphed into a cold, snarly, panda eyed drug freak. It pains me to this day that in his search for new beginnings, he found me and the Numb, mercilessly driven towards our own destiny.

Rex got bad, near psychotic, to the point where we all got concerned for him and his rocking the political boat. His dysfunction should have been the semtex bomb to blow all this bullshit to hell, giving us all a chance of salvation. But that would be hypocritical, I stated the rules of engagement, we were all big boys now, and not even Rex falling apart at the seams could release me from my desire to protect the group.

I was a drug addict, I didn't want to baby-sit a guy who burned himself out, I didn't want to feel responsible for the destruction of his undeniable talent, but there was always the dehumanizing qualification that we all knew what we were getting into.

The reality couldn't have been further from the truth. We all arrived relatively green, Rex just more so. He turned into a fiend, that could be accepted, still manageable by the construct, but he also turned into a washed up, manic depressed, born again drug free Christian. Again great for Rex but disastrous for the group.

So with all this said and done all the parties, drugs and bullshit, I was left with Trent as my wingman. Sophie was long gone emotionally, even though I was unaware of this. So could Trent and I continue? Well I had a trip planned to go back to England for a few weeks, so I guess the cards would fall where they may and control would be suspended.

✹ ✹ ✹

My return to England was overpowered by the nagging Numb and its pedantry and dogma concerning what still lay in NYC. My poor family, I must have looked like shit, emotionally bankrupt, devoid of any tangible sentimentality, because with things as shaky as they were in New York, opening my heart to the wholesome love that was there for me was impossible. Rather than rewarding my parents, who I was bleeding dry financially with my exploits, with stories of how I had done this great scene that was seen by some big shot, I showed up flaky and shallow. They just wanted to see a spark of the person they loved. A glimpse beyond the pain I was encapsulated in, a voice to tear down the self-manipulating lies I used as my New York mantras, a way to feel my love. I was in a shell, unbreakable, and the Numb wanted me closer to annihilation before I was allowed the sun to shine on my face again. I was not oblivious to nature, the tear in my mum's eye, the worry

The Numb and Me and Green Trainers

of my dad, but it was all refractions of truth through the broken prism of numbness and addiction.

As hard as it must have been for them, a meat bag facsimile, a doppelganger of me had made that transatlantic trip, but in essence it would be some time before they would see love in their son's eyes again.

I remember glorifying Sophie and showing off about how lucky I was. Due to the illicit and occult world that I lived and breathed, it was almost impossible to talk to Mum and Dad or Joy about anything. The dogma of the drug culture politique was too prevalent in everything I did. Even the pain of not being able to connect with the one's I loved could not break the grim hold addiction held over me, and the chaos of my American life.

I spent a lot of time wanting to buy presents for all the old chums. What would they want, except for drugs, and half of them had quit? I realized I knew nothing about the guys, nothing at all, except some would and some wouldn't want drugs as a present and taking this in to account I guess it was nothing all round. Oh, but there was my dear sweet Sophie. I asked Mum if she could shell out on a bottle of expensive perfume, she did, and a pretty necklace, yes again, and so on.

I was going back to New York to continue with the life. Thanks Mum, Dad and Joy, sorry for being a vacuous bastard but no, it wouldn't have even crossed my mind that I was so inglorious. I only had clues to go on that flashed in my migraine nightmares, then reset.

So back to New York: straight to the apartment, Sophie looking sullen on the bed, "I know what will cheer you up", presents unpacked and given; the gossamer film of Mum's decency and kindness irking me, Sophie's mood worse now, a pain in my chest, something weird was going on, am I going to die, seven days cold turkey or guilt dangling from Mum's tear, in a strange mood, Sophie close to tears, started me actually feeling rational emotion, "no, I can't accept these", Sophie's crying.

"What's going on here, this isn't exactly the response I was hoping for", no response.

Watching the scaly tears roll down her cheek I thought, bad timing girl. It was a little too close to my nagging sense of guilt about walking away from a family in tears.

I'd seen Sophie cry before, she was an actress, and this episode felt like a sham.

My mind was doing back flips, pirouettes and triple salkos whilst juggling some very pointy venomous daggers. I'm no juggler, acrobat, dancer or ice skater so with all the daggers falling appropriately into my back I lay on the floor with my green trainers on, the Numb snarling in anticipation.

"Did you do anything while I was away?"

"What do you mean", in a window of common sense I could smell this rat a mile off, I needed to be concise, leave no room for a barrage of fiction to confuse me; I may have been somewhat clear headed but not entirely. I needed to keep this simple.

"Sophie look at me", her eyes fixed upon the threadbare carpet I noticed as filthy for the first time,

"Sophie, did you fuck someone when I was gone", no response.

"Well did you?" Seeing tears streaming down her face angered me, I was working my self up into a rage that was neutralized instantly when my eyes surveyed the half opened gift, chosen with greed, paid for by a mothers love. This rendered me tender, insecure heart decimated, tramped on again.

"Sophie"

"Trent"

"What Trent, you . . . Trent." I couldn't believe it, he was my friend. But, I must remember things as they were then, not now with this burst of clarity. We were only drug friends in a political utilitarian symbiosis if I remembered. Oh no, had my master plan fallen apart? Had the fragility of my group been put under too much pressure and imploded as a response to my temporary separation? I guess this was the end. The group had contrived a way to disintegrate and to shatter like this. I didn't deserve better, what did I say, he gave nothing emotionally, you know the rest. The Numb stroked me, so this was my lesson: throughout all this I got lost up my own ass, and life had this inevitable treat waiting for me, my only friend screwing my girlfriend, what a cut throat way to learn, when,

"No it's not like you think."

"I don't want to think about it at all."

"No you don't understand."

"Well fuckin spell it out!"

"He forced me."

Oh my god, Fred Wilson time again. Sophie was not to be trusted, almost everything in the last six months had been based on convenience and lies, but how could I live with myself if my gut feeling that she was full of shit was wrong. I told her "wait here, I'm going to sort this out."

Euan Sutton

By the time I tracked Trent down, he was in a state of submissiveness; he knew I could be scrappy, as he knew he could, and I think was ready to get it over with.

I called Steve, in my desperation, I had him and one other person I knew from a different group, Carl. With the total collapse of all I thought I knew, these two were my options; returning home at this point was not. Steve said he'd have Trent's kneecaps blown out; I despite my anger was not turned on to violence, so declined. He said "anything you need, call." Yeah, been down that road.

So there was Carl, almost a complete stranger but a man who would prove to become my new friend in a new circle, no politics, no dogma this time. Yeah right.

But for the situation with Sophie and Trent: He was prepared to take a beating for his indiscretions, but he had no idea of what Sophie had accused him of.

It became so clear that Sophie had lied to avoid conflict with me; she must have either cared a little for me, or just was ruthless enough to have Trent bare the weight of it.

The story played out like this. Sophie, bored with me gone went down to see Spike and Trent. She was always a hopeless flirt, and apparently was that night too. I figured that with Spike and Rex doing their own things, and the rules we lived by, any sense of loyalty would be absurd. Sophie and Trent got high; Sophie gave Trent head, end of story.

But for the reaction of Trent, he was floored, not with a punch but with a spear of true emotion, straight through his soul, which must have mirrored my absolute sadness. He even said, "go on hit me I deserve it". There was no energy left for me to do it. I didn't really feel angry anyway. The Numb saw to that and showed the whole dysfunctional episode for what it was: the right conclusion to a bad situation. When you stop caring about people and you're around them long enough, and you replace friendship with usefulness, then somebody's gonna get hurt. In this case we all got hurt, when humanity reared its untimely head. But as for now, where the hell was I going to sleep tonight.

✻ ✻ ✻

I had been in New York for over a year and had nothing to show for my time except my two suitcases packed in anticipation for my return to England, housing their innards like a time capsule for the pre-headfuck, girlfriend losing, friendship ending episode that had just come to pass. My cumulative experiences both good and bad were piling up like a mountain of festering garbage choking the air, depriving deep breath, yet left somehow alone, amounting to problems that I would eventually get around to avoiding.

And then there was Carl. It was a massive reach to call and ask for his support: in support I mean accommodation. We barely knew each other and he moved in different circles to me and my old gang of *out of sight out of mind* traitorous turncoats.

Even taking in to account that I probably deserved what had happened to me I was still smarting from the way my life had changed, without consent or agreement, rationality or humanity. I had become a control freak out of control with a mind numbing obsessive fixation on how I had got shafted so badly. This is the time when you need your friends or family for support. With my family obviously worried about my continuing exploration of New York after such clear errors in judgment, going home seemed a plausible option to them. My return must have looked inevitable; I was a complete wreck with apparently no card left to play. I did however have one last wild card: to ask a stranger for help.

So, I called up Carl. He was at the Academy but part of the morning class. You see the first year was divided in half between the morning guys and us, or what used to be us, in the afternoon.

There was a semi-healthy rivalry between the two sections at the beginning of the year but as the party life began to take over the morning guys seemed less relevant. Maybe if I had have been placed in the morning crew I would have been a different, more productive young actor. We could afford to stay up way past our bedtimes because we didn't have to be coherent until midday; the other guys had to be alert by 9am so were mostly normal in their work/party balance. I would find out shortly that the morning guys saw us as a bunch of drugged up good for nothings. We were actually considered un-cool by these guys. A week ago I would have been unable to conceive of this and would have fought tooth and nail to protect the evening lad's lifestyle and image. But now there was nothing left to defend, just hollow imitations of self styled gods.

Carl was one of the morning guys, which made things awkward. This was not the only problem. He was one of the elite from the morning intake. He was at the epicenter of morning cool with sidekicks flanking him. These two were called Laars and Tom. I would later learn that very similar extra curricular activities were

The Numb and Me and Green Trainers

being explored by some of the morning guys. They were simply better at keeping their cards closer to their chests. With nothing to lose I called Carl and remarkably was invited to join him and his ensemble crowd at his new studio apartment situated just off Park Avenue South. With my head swimming with self-deprecation I toted my suitcases down to where he lived. I pressed the buzzer to the apartment on a nice looking building. The buzzer croaked out, "Yeh, who is it?"
I said, "Wil."
"Wil, huh, Wil who? Hey let me just . . . ."
The buzzer fell silent. Oh great, how far I had fallen in a matter of one day. I pressed the buzzer again.
"Yeh, hello", replied a new voice.
I said, "Hi, its Wil. I just spoke to . . . ."
"Oh, Wil, you wanna come up?"
No shit, I thought to myself but this was no time for ego, "Yes, if it's ok."
BBBDZZZZZZZA. Someone in the apartment had pressed the door release buzzer that in turn had granted me access in to the hallway. However with my cases slowing me down I couldn't get to the door in time. After taking stock of the slapstick nature of the situation I positioned my bags as close as possible to the door ready to pounce through. But the door stayed silent. Obviously the people upstairs were having a sufficiently good time to have ten second attention spans and no temporal awareness. I found in me the pool of humility: bent over and took a look in the reflection. Yes, I was a sorry sight, but I was in need to take a drink if I was to survive this experience. I lowered myself closer and closer with trepidation, and then a big slapstick boot materialized from nowhere and gave me an almighty

kick in the ass sending me head over heels in to the pool. After swallowing most of the humility reservoir I pressed the door buzzer again.
"Yeh, who is", eventually rang out with the tone of what could have been the first person that had answered the buzzer or a third person.
"Er, it's Wil."
"Who?"
"I'm here to see Carl . . . ." There were a few seconds of the static white noise dripping out of the door mechanism along with a few barely discernable party noises in the background and then nothing. This couldn't have been a more embarrassingly un-cool entrance. I thought about turning away, but to what? This was it, life in all its glory. So if ridicule was on the menu I was due extra helpings. With every miscommunication I moved closer to social excommunication. Then there was a shout, not from the grate in the wall but from above.
"Hey!"
I looked up then down again quickly, the sun was bright in the sky and ensured that the owner of the voice remained a mystery.
"Hey", I heard a sense of fun in the voice from above, "what are you still doing down there?"
"I just missed the . . . ."
"What, can't here you. Laars, turn the music down. What are you still doing down there?"
A calm breeze whispered to me as I craned my neck and momentarily bathed in the sunlight without a care in the world. In a muffled tone I could hear what sounded like distant voices from another dimension, "Carl, that kid's still down there" then,

The Numb and Me and Green Trainers

Bdzzzzzza. I reached forward as if in a dream and was immediately ushered back into reality. Without warning the door latch was released by the upstairs gizmo and I made my way through the doors. Shit, there was another set of internal doors. They were buzzing also. I lunged for the interior door and grabbed one of my cases to prop it open. With one suitcase still hanging out on the street and one in the doorway I became lost in the whole arseholeness of the situation again. Why? Why did the simple job of getting in to the one lifeline I had left in NYC resemble a scene from a comedy routine; no humor though, no final pratfall. There was only one task to execute: Just open the outside door, grab the case, pull it inside, take both cases through the interior door and then and only then could I go about asking a stranger for lodgings after making a complete twat of myself. The building had an elevator; couldn't work it. Won't go into it right now but it had something to do with closing inner and outer doors, a topic of which I had received my daily dose. So I was in then promptly out of the elevator with the two increasingly heavy cases, and made my way up the marble staircase. Clitter Clatter Clomp Clitter Clatter Klomp was the song of the two cases as I awkwardly climbed the three flights of stairs. I then finally arrived at the door to the apartment; well I assumed it was the right door. With the drama of the last thirty minutes it felt like more of a guess than a certainty that I was in the right place. Then a wave of pride hit me. It was not a machismo swagger, moreover an indignant scowl focused through the door numbers to the people inside. A few days ago I had been 'the man', now only phantoms of my princely status remained and needled me, "why should these morning class wanabees make a mockery of me"? With a sense of righteous indignation I went to wrap on the door, it pushed open.

I saw a tall good-looking bloke standing in the kitchen. He spotted me in the doorway and said, "Wanna a drink?"

"Watcha got", I replied in a semi sarcastic affected voice. It sounded good in my head to respond to the first question asked in a kind of John Wayne-esque fashion as if I was going in to a Wild West saloon expecting a gunfight. Luckily for me all this was lost on the self-styled bartender. He was distracted, looking at an assortment of bottles crammed in to the tiny kitchen like a person searching for a library book. He said, "Margaritas". I was not big in to cocktails, well at least alcoholic ones. But I definitely had an itch that needed scratching and drugs were obviously off the list today. I mean in the circumstances that may have been a little too much to expect, don't ya think? I assumed by the European accent that the bartender *de moment* was Laars. Laars was accepted as an alpha in the morning set. He had a rather lofty superior attitude to what he considered as kids games. He shunned most of the people in our collective groups engendering an exclusivity of his time that in turn made people want to gain his acceptance. There were people who tried to hang all over him but failed. Carl and Tom were the only people Laars saw as peers. So bags down I walked up to collect my drink. Drink; must have a cigarette, "Can we smoke in here?"

"No, no, outside on the balcony".

As I walked the fifteen feet from the kitchen to the window, via the entire length of the apartment two things became apparent. One, it was not a balcony it

The Numb and Me and Green Trainers

was a fire escape and two, the studio had no furniture in it at all. So I climbed out of the window drink in hand.

"Hey what up dude. I'm Tom". Ok so this was Tom, the second element to this social triumvirate. "Drinking the Margaritas hey?"

"Yes, got given to me."

"Cool, cool."

"Do you mind if I smoke?"

"No dude that's cool."

"You don't drink the cocktails Tom?"

"Yeh, if I have to. Right now I've got myself a brew, well did have. I'm going to get another beer, you want one?"

"Sure but if we're having a beer shouldn't we have a shot? I mean we've got the tequila".

"Holy shit English I can't argue with that". So I downed my Margarita, it was ok but now we were cooking. I didn't know these guys from a hole in the wall but we had chanced upon a common area in which I could emerge highly talented; drinking. One thing I found out early on living in the States was that if you were British you were expected to be able to drink a lot. I was in this new environment for ten minutes and had already had a quick cocktail, a beer and a shot of tequila. It was as my neck snapped back to facilitate the downing of the shot that I saw Carl up close and personal for the first time.

Had I fucked up big time? I mean it's one thing for Carl's friends to party hard in his new place but what about me? Could my hardcore reputation from before be enough to excuse my excess here?

Carl said, "What's up". That was it, no profundity just a simple greeting. He had emerged from the one room in the diminutive apartment that I had not yet ventured into; the bathroom. I replied, "Not much man, want a shot?

Bang!

The coin was in the air. If Carl said no, it would be the end of my NYC life. It would clearly show early disapproval for me on good behavior and logically close any doors to me in my more 'natural' state of being. If he said yes well maybe, maybe . . . we should just cut to the chasers. "Sure. Laars" Carl said in a heavily affected way. He may have been taking the piss or it may have been a sign of endearment. Either way it made me feel better. "Laars, you in?"

"OK".

So that was that. Three friends and a stranger drinking shots with chasers prior to any attempts at real conversation. The shots went down well, was handed a forty-ounce as a chaser. Well time to step up. I felt a test was being set.

"Tom", the name flowed from my lips like we were best buds, "you want to go smoke?" Without being asked Carl was the first through on the balcony/fire-escape with me following with Tom next. Got my smokes out and started to hand them around. Everybody had a pack but I wanted to bring something to the table. I had given nothing to the group so far and found this as the moment. Without acknowledgement the smokes were taken from me. A book of matches was pulled out, the type that are given away when you buy a pack, the type that go out with any hint of a breeze. Tom took the matches, did this folding trick with the cardboard, lit

The Numb and Me and Green Trainers

his smoke first then Carl's then blew the flame out. Was this the first in a long line of actions designed to put me in my place? No, Tom was superstitious and went on about the one regarding the soldiers in World War One: the first strike, spot: second strike, sighted and zeroed in on; third strike, I said, "you're out". With the beer and liquor flowing I felt like attempting humor; bad move. I was not known well enough to make light of Tom's intensely over dramatic portrayal of life for the snipers of The Great War. He didn't know that I had heard this old chestnut before so he just took it as a noisy interruption. Carl was expressionless as Tom almost seamlessly finished the story after telling it again from the beginning. I asked him to pass the matches. Without the special folding trick to aid ignition I had only luck on my side. The day had conspired to be mostly embarrassingly emasculating thus far. Was lighting this cigarette going to turn into a fiasco; another anecdote invoked to remember the ghosts of those who were snuffed out by the Manhattan machine? My anxiety was dispelled as I attempted to light the crucial third match. Carl grunted and handed me his lit cigarette to light from. "Thanks", no reply.

It was easy to forget the big question looming over the whole day: the matter of my potential homelessness. With the tequila flowing freely only into shot glasses and beer being guzzled I felt that I had rapidly graduated out of the freshman ranks that had applied to me a few hours earlier. My mind raced. Had all this been a one off dose of boredom relief for my present company? Would my alcoholic excesses be debated *in absentia* and be used to black ball me from future social events? Would my presence be used to exemplify hang over headaches, next day nausea and short tempers and become a footnote to the usury and a touchstone to the superficial? Luckily, it wouldn't be long before my position in this new scene would be cemented and my paranoia would be eased.

Laars and Tom were flat mates together in a dump in Alphabet City on the Lower East Side. They served a miscellany of functions for one another: confidant and co-con man when substantiating each other stories and wingman when they were out scouting for ladies.

I wondered whether Carl was a loner who had invited his only acquaintances to share in an impromptu house warming or the leader of this small pack, calling upon and dismissing his loyal subjects with the confidence of someone in complete control.

Well it got to that time in the evening when everyone felt it was probably time to go. As Tom and Laars grabbed their shoulder bags my eyes were drawn to my cases. I looked at them wondering whether I would have to push these guys for a piece of floor at their apartment as Carl acclimatized to life in his new place. It had slipped my mind to ask Carl if I could stay with him and at this point it all seemed too late. I stood up and shuffled around a bit. I was not making a real effort to leave nor was I fully staying. As Tom and Laars said their goodbyes to Carl and me, I sensed the inevitable goodbye I would soon be making to Carl and subsequently New York. I was not prepared to move my shit to another random place so I began to reconcile to myself that this time it was truly over. My thoughts were babbling as I stood now motionless in the empty studio with Carl's large frame acting as the only furniture. Then came a voice, "Why don't you take a seat."

I replied, "yeh but the guys are leaving."
"They know where they're going. Take a seat."
"Well it's a shame for you to have to sit here alone on your house-warming".
I sat. We talked about a lot of stuff. He already knew about the whole deal that I was up to my neck in. He said, "You don't mind sleeping on the floor do you?"
"Are you sure?"
"It's only a floor."
With that out the way we began talking some more. I felt a little uncertain about this outstanding generosity but went with it.
I opened my case to pull out a sweater to lean against and to my horror out popped The Numb. With the frenetic pace of the last few days coupled with my desperation I had temporarily forgotten about this skulking menace. I started getting pissed off with the timing of this entrance. Why could the Numb have not surfaced a few days ago when I really needed a release? Why come now? This did not bode well. I thought the day had gone a little too well. So why, Numb? Why were you there uninvited? The party had been good. I had probably beaten the odds and found a way to stay in the city so why turn up now? This new scene seemed safe enough. Yeh, no crazy doings, just life. I thought I would be able to unpack my baggage and heal some of the pain. You were there for a reason, you always were, so what was it?
There were never any direct answers just annoying naggings.
Not now.

I needed some rest, some sanity, a break from the cruelness, but my un-welcome mentor of unsavory teachings obviously had other ideas.

There would be no rest, no time to slack off from truth finding: that bitch that makes our forever-binding trip back to the Danger Station, platform whatever.

So there we were, the three us at the point of going onwards. It was weird having an anonymous silent voice at the best of times but there around Carl it felt doubly strange. Carl had a spooky quality, silent and still, that felt like x-ray specs to the Numb one. If this was indeed a reality then it was time to take stock of the situation and see whether it was truth mission over or in need of some new planning. Maybe Carl had no supernatural powers to detect my special pal. If not he certainly knew how to harness the power of silence and wield it in a way that tested you. If you suck all the oxygen out of a room and stand back to watch, you quickly see who panics, who fights and who resigns themselves to their fate; in the same way Carl could suffocate you with silence. This could draw out secrets, hidden agendas and lies. I felt that honesty was the best policy with Carl though the Numb had to remain a secret. I guess that every time it showed up around Carl it would risk exposure. But the Numb was afraid of nothing or no one so it was anyone's guess how this was going to work out.

I felt really tired, no, exhausted. It had been quite a week emotionally with a long boozy day tacked on the end. I was talking with Carl about this and that but my mind was getting lost in an opaque concrete maze. It was only the residual adrenalin from the shock to my system from looking down the barrel of destitution that kept me propped upright against the empty floor.

For the first time in ages childlike warmth overcame me. I felt that I was sliding in my thoughts and soul chatter. Remembering the starry night of my unglamorous snowboarding accident I conjured up my bed at Monastery House and wanted to drift, floating along with the sounds of New York nurturing me like a soothing lullaby from the bosom of the city that never sleeps.

As I went further in to the open arms of Morpheus I remembered how I first viewed Manhattan, with its glitz and party packed pace maker lifestyle. Now I wondered if the City's moniker was a misunderstood curse. The idea of eternal go and no rest, no sleep held no attraction. I was attempting to pay attention to Carl if he was indeed talking. Maybe he wasn't. But, as I made eye contact with him for the first time in maybe a half hour, I saw his lips move and felt a wrenching churning feeling from my stomach. Had I misread the situation, the hollow echoes of words would not enable me to differentiate vague pleasantries from a horrible dream. My teeth were clamped together wanting to grind but for the power of my lock-jawed bite. I felt that I had been blindfolded then spun around maybe twenty times then released in to a room full of nightmares. Carl's words were out of sync with his lips at first; these first words that thrusted my body into a state of red alert. Strangely the Numb was trying to soothe me: Stop.

The falling sensation came crashing to a halt with the impact of a runaway elevator colliding with the ground. The air blowing in from the window now felt cold. I felt the presence of a creeping hangover and with it confusion. My senses felt alive in opposition to my dead weight body. I could feel my legs and bum; they were sore with all the sitting. I managed to get to my feet and shake off what felt like a deep freeze sensation. I quickly found a cigarette, lit it, it tasted disgusting but I carried on smoking it anyway. I saw people walking by outside and wondered if their lives were better than mine.

"So how about it?"

Please if I tap my heels three times I'll be sucked out of the window, down the fire escape with my tongue hanging out of my mouth licking the scum off of the sidewalks of New York en-route to the Atlantic where I would be washed clean with an oceanic salt scrub to land flat on my back in my childhood bed at Monastery House; this imaginary journey governed by an invisible force enforcing one last taste of shit before granting me clemency and offering freedom. But freedom from what dammit!? Me that's fucking what: no more Numb, no more filth, no more insomnia. But I'd be the same there wouldn't I? What about my will power? Was that the force giving me a glimpse of another life, a life back with my loved ones, or had my willpower given way to desperation and therefore showing the clear fiction of a life now beyond my grasp.

"Well?"

I felt my head lolling to one side, there was no way I could avoid Carl's question any longer. Saying nothing was wearing thin and even though I was lost in thought a part of me knew the question being asked. Moreover I knew that there was only one answer that would be heard.

I would have no sleep ever again.

"So can we call him?"

The Numb and Me and Green Trainers

This may have been the last chance to avoid the total immersion baptism of fire. I stood rooted to the spot knowing that my heart was breaking in two.

I wanted to know everything about life, people and humanity. I wanted to trust life wherever it took me. Well life, here I was again, rooted to the spot, realizing that throughout my journey I had never fully let go, except on the slopes of the Blue Ridge Mountains with my head-butting contest with a chair lift. I had exceeded most people's party perimeters to the tune of addiction but with just my head above water I was still breathing the same air as everyone else. I was still demanding the basic principles of life that most people lived by and finally I, along with most of humanity, was not prepared to fully let go.

"Well can we or not?"

My hand was held out in front of me seemingly governed by a separate brain. In my outstretched arm there were highly strung fingers holding a business card.

I looked at my tattooed arm wondering what it would be like to be a baby version of myself. Was I ever really innocent? The day in the schoolyard: my reaction, the Numb, back to being a baby tattooed and crying for help, green trainers on, desperately trying to kick one off and equally trying to hold one on with all of my might.

What was I growing into? I think this question would have to be put on ice.

I finally said,

"Go ahead. Dial the Number. When you hear the beep dial 666. When he calls back to arrange the drop I'll speak to him. How much do you want?"

I'd never sleep again.

The conflict of emotions felt at that moment would echo through my thoughts for years. Unfortunately with no distance or room to see the big picture the microscopic space of the studio apartment was being shrink-wrapped in to an addiction-fuelled claustrophobia. The glimmer of hope was a true mirage to my thirst for sobriety and normalcy. I felt as if I was being dragged out to sea, frightened by the prospect of drowning alone but eagerly anticipating an end to this miserable existence. The cocaine high would magically lift me up out of the swirling current only to view the stormy waters beneath a sunless sky. I would inevitably be plunged back down in to the black water carrying too much weight to stay afloat as flotsam and jetsam and sink like an anchor to my own life boat.

With the weight of my burden bearing down on the compound fracture that existed between my soul and the urgency of breathing, feelings surged through my body ending in my fingers as I took the phone from Carl and awaited the call from my friendly neighborhood drug dealer.

The deed was getting done and with that the phoenix persona of the Numb emerged resplendent against the backdrop of my ashened life.

Before I knew it I was almost dead.

It's like walking through a membrane or walking in to a sci-fi dimension, just not as profound or sexy. You know you're doing wrong. You're feet turn to lead with no amphetamine solution. With senses tingling you are arguably more alive than ever before. With every step forward you strip back layers of innocence with a roaring ferocity akin to the red nose of a shuttle. With the launcher fulfilling its hedonistic duty to relentlessly push onwards before dying out, rejected, to become cold space debris.

How could I have been expected to relish the artifice of a stage school stage when my heart and soul were being consumed by life in NYC?

Surging onwards at a snails pace my body started to feel fundamentally at odds with my brain and distant from any moral touchstone. I knew I was poisoning myself. I didn't feel indestructible. There was no poignancy or epiphany just schism.

There was something unnatural about reckless abandonment, a lack of compassion and selfish self-destruction. But, increasingly, that's all I saw in myself and others.

By now I had developed a perverse symbiotic relationship between the Numb, the drug dealer and me. As dirty and base as the relationship was it felt good. To have somebody reliable in your life was refreshing. Friends could be made and lost in the twinkling of an eye yet JJ, as I will call the point of the triangle, the one-man drug emporium, was always there. All you had to do was call.

As the call was made the parts of me left with any emotional buoyancy twinged with excitement and anticipation. There was no real satisfaction, happiness or contentment but I had learned to replace these wholesome tenets with far more accessible alternatives. The overriding feeling that hit me was that of being cool. I looked back on the pseudo-dangerous characters at Langley and Postville and smirked. Here I was hanging out with the real deal at the bargain price of about $100 per visit.

Beepers were a requisite part of life for all of us. We all had them despite their sole purpose of arranging parties and drug taking. After JJ was paged I sat back and waited. This waiting was an essential part of the process: Is he going to get the page? Is he going to make the drop? When he comes will he have the right stuff?

Sometimes you would wait for a long time; sometimes you were left waiting into the anxious early morning of the next day. It could be 3am and you would have resigned yourself to a night of drinking and smoking trippy weed. You would barely have the energy to answer the phone but you knew you had to. The choice then would be yours: Would you shift gears and put your foot on the gas or drift away into relaxation? Either way it was good to receive 'the call'. There were a few times that you would never be called back. These were the worst. Your universe condensed in to an atmosphere impossible to live and breathe in. You'd feel dejected, stood up by the best looking girl in the world who had promised that tonight would be 'the night'. It was awful, but the blame was interestingly never laid at JJ's feet. It was simply understood that you were not always in the driving seat.

The initial few calls to JJ were met with anxiety and wariness but not now. I had dialed in my return number and did not wait long till the phone rang. Carl looked on with eager anticipation as I said "just a $50 sack."
"Ok."
"Yeh, an hour is fine."
"Oh, I'm living somewhere new."

The Numb and Me and Green Trainers

At this point things got a little frosty, any change to the status quo was poorly received, but I had earned a degree of trust, well, as much as would be given to a customer, so after giving my new address, it was time to sit back and make small talk with Carl. This was the first time we were sharing an uncomfortable silence.

Of the many things to be afraid of the biggest fear that I tried to blot out was the realization that we have a choice in life.

There is a truth in accepting responsibility for our actions. There is however a truth in running away. We can easily get all Zen about my predicament, 'where there is darkness there is always light' and 'vice versa', well I chose dark for now, it didn't hurt my eyes as much. Sitting there in silence my spirits were lifted when I saw my new favorite item of Carl's furniture, a four foot round glass table; I could barely contain my excitement as the door buzzer alerted us to feeding time, Pavlov's dogs never felt like this. Yes, we were salivating and excitable, just like the dogs, the difference was that our appetite would never be sated. The door buzzer was like the starting pistol for the rest of our lives, not merely an attempt to satisfy our ravenous appetites. All of a sudden I started to panic. Yeh we were about to get high, but what about afterwards, after all the party juice was gone. I could remember my licked fingers mopping up dust on the floor around the vicinity of our snorting in a vain attempt to defeat the coming down. Would I do that this time? I was agonizing over the point of getting high knowing that I would have to come crashing down; the miserable silence that follows the uber-interesting philosophizing, music, et al; the golden melodies of any music that passes your ears becoming fingers being dragged down a chalkboard. Any interaction with other people transforms into hard labor; in a nutshell coming down was no fun. But I had no choice, right? I needed to get high to resuscitate my monochromatic life with an injection of color. The downside was the bleaching out of life's interest post-party, but I guess it was worth it. The adage, 'it's better to have got high and then crashed than to never have got high at all', flooded in to me. It was going to be ok.

I got to the door. Carl was unknown to JJ and there was the whole thing about trust, so I jubilantly went onwards, like a trusted knight, with battle scars and consequent respect.

JJ said, "nice place" then saw Carl. They exchanged glances.

JJ said, "here's the $50 bag."

Carl intervened and said, "can I get two of those?"

Like a trainers delight in breaking in a stallion, the tension evaporated and acceptance beckoned.

JJ said, "for a $100 I can give you this"; he proceeded to pull out a bag with what looked like a small solid sucking candy. I looked again to the glass table and the bag, Carl ponied up the cash, we received the goods, JJ was offered the mandatory cup of tea, he declined like usual and said his goodbyes or more accurately grunted, "see ya later" then left. What was left was a big invitation to begin the party. Carl took the solid ball out of the bag and shook the loose powder onto the glass table. There was more than first anticipated. Carl cut two lines down the center of the table and said, "want to race?" I didn't need any further reason. All feeling of fear, anxiety or trepidation drifted over the horizon

like a distant memory, in a way that gave hope to them never returning.
I tested my vacuumesque nostrils, they were in fine order so with no further ado, it was time to raise the curtain. I huffed the coke up, a little flew into the back of my throat, which felt good. The petroleum taste was in itself not great, I mean some people like the smell of petrol when filling their car, but they would not douse themselves with it. The coke taste was not great but as a by-product to sucking up a huge line it was pleasant and numbing. After the first line of the day, it was time for a well earned cigarette, but with hygiene out the window, I licked my finger and dragged it down the beautiful white outline of what was there before, a sad soulful reminder of beauty, like an angelic skid mark. I daubed the remnants around my gums, felt the tingle, looked over at Carl, he grinned, I grinned, I passed him a smoke, he lit a match, ignited my cigarette, then his own then said, "how about another?"

Well there was another and another and so on. The fabric of my life was acquiring a new set of stains. It was a little too easy to slip back into the old pair of shoes. The idea of a new life in new shiny shoes was only in its embryonic stages yet already pinched and engendered a feeling of separation anxiety. For the next couple of weeks things remained about the same as the first night. The only thing that changed was the increasing amount of furniture that sprung up in the apartment. Living with Carl was cool. With the exception of having to listen to either Frank Sinatra or Dean Martin constantly, Carl and I agreed on most things. A typical day would involve getting up around noon at the earliest, as Carl had strayed away from his Academy duties, citing a need for convalescence, grabbing a beer or can of soda for breakfast followed by a couple of cigarettes. Sinatra would be singing his heart out. This was not as soothing as you might imagine when considering that the night before the same songs were with me and my drug induced insomnia. Hearing the words, "it was a very good year" over the top of Carl's snoring failed to soften my lockjaw and permanent headache. So with the CD playing in a loop I would suggest that a trip to a diner was already overdue. I would never feel hungry but the idea of an endless cup of coffee and a break from the crooning was alluring. It always took Carl forever to get ready so I would often substitute a further cigarette with a small spliff or a hit from a wonderfully ornate glass pipe. The idea was usually better than the actual event; the reason for this was that the weed that we got was strong, in fact too strong to really be enjoyed. The weed was acquired to act as a sedative. Some of the uptown professionals that we came into contact with were happy to pop diazepam on a nightly basis to take the edge off of the day; we preferred a natural remedy. Having a morning smoke spelt laziness for the entire day to follow. That was of course until I powdered my nose in the evening. The trip to the diner was usually uneventful but the coffee and cigarettes were so soothing. I enjoyed the sunshine on my face especially as the temperature fell. The crisp air flooding the diner, the hum of the street having the volume turned up and down as customers came and went, all held together by the molasses brain glue inhaled earlier. The time to leave was usually marked by an overflowing little black ashtray. Strewn amongst the fully smoked butts there were full cigarettes, rendered unsmokable by the little pool of water left at the bottom of the ashtray after an unsympathetic quick swill by the incredibly busy waiters.

After breakfast Carl and I would either walk around aimlessly for a while or head back to the apartment for a quick blast of crooning and a smoke. Carl managed to have a much busier schedule than me. I found it difficult when in amongst the abject laziness an injection of purposefulness would emerge and prompt Carl to go off and do something useful. This was especially difficult to accept when the task was acting related. It cut a little near the nerves to be reminded of the real purpose of being in New York. It was interesting that despite the deadening of most common sense I still had it in me to feel a pang of guilt regarding the disparity between my decadence and my poor family who were funding it. As shameful as it is though, this clear sense of guilt was short-lived and usually quickly masked by anything that The Numb would steer me to. The after breakfast mood was usually pretty somber. The absence of sleep at night meant that after the initial flurry of energy that I could muster immediately after waking up was depleted, I would feel spent. I must reiterate that by spent I mean totally exhausted mentally, emotionally and physically. The sleep deprivation and failure to ever eat properly meant that my body had stopped responding to normal protocol and instead operated exclusively to a cocaine timetable. All time outside of partying was distorted and somehow irrelevant. There seemed to be a clear demarcation between the time when drinking and smoking weed was permitted and the time that we would start with the coke. We constructed a kind of rule that held the daytime with a degree of respect. Only on very naughty and willfully self-indulgent occasions would we start with the serious shit in the morning 'cos we knew that once we started we would keep on going and going for as long as we had a stash. It would almost certainly mean that there would be more than one phone call to JJ. The first phone call would have an element of reasoning to it. A calculation would be made, an equation based around the following factors: time, opportunity and stamina. The most important factor was always left unaccounted for: addiction. However you planned it, there would never be enough. The only reason I attempted to sleep was that the drugs had all been used up and it was either too late to call JJ or I had run out of money. The second phone call resembled a rabid dog baying for blood. There was no common sense involved; my dark desires were in the driving seat with the Numb in the passenger seat enjoying the ride. So starting early was generally a bad idea; there would be all the physical symptoms associated with over snorting, the worst being the ubiquitous gummed-up nostrils.

The rest of the afternoon, that would have been spent hanging out with Spike or Trent, were now taken up with staring out of the window or lolling about on the fire escape smoking. By about 5pm the pit in my stomach would be desperate for some counterbalance to the acid wash it was swilling around. I couldn't face anything too stodgy but thin crust pizza nearly always sounded good. I would usually force down a couple of slices along with a can of coke or two. There was one occasion that I woke up at pizza time and placed the

The Numb and Me and Green Trainers

order but lacked the energy to get out of bed to answer the door buzzer a half an hour later, good times.
And then there was the evening; a carbon copy of the day's jaunts just with the lights turned out.

I woke up one day to the usual serenade of snoring, farting and 'fly me to the moon'. The air felt very heavy, I felt clammy and anxious and disgusted by the debris from the night before. There were the usual chalky white stains on the table smeared by the saliva and finger combo. There was the split open, empty baggy that had once held semi-satisfying medicine, now licked clean and clearly pointing an accusatorial finger at me. There were empty pizza boxes all over the floor, a product of many days munching. Pizza boxes always piled up because they wouldn't fit down the garbage shoot and required manual transportation to the basement. Not a big deal you might say but remember the other pizza related incident when I couldn't even prize myself out of bed. There was an open pizza box on the table with a few gnawed-on crusts left behind. There were gallons worth of empty coke cans and bottles, empty beer bottles some with warm beer still inside that would often splash all over everywhere as you lost concentration in the clear up. Some of the bottles were more reminiscent of ashtrays than anything else. Even though it was a non-smoking apartment there were now obvious concessions to the rules. In the miniature kitchen every plate, glass and mug was dirty.
I made my way to the bathroom with arachnid like trepidation and nearly gagged at the stench of the toilet, used and unflushed, and mildewed. The towels in the bathroom always stunk and reminded me of my

delicious towel at Postville. Despite the smell the water in the shower was always scalding and poured out of the old fashioned spout with a pounding ferocity that could on occasion be unpleasant. That day it felt a little painful but refreshing all the same. It was grim to dry myself with a stinky, damp, moldy towel but I was preoccupied with a sense of anticipation about the day ahead. I got dressed and felt a little weak and wobbly; not so much because of the excesses of the night before, I was used to this, but because I had hardly slept a wink.

The steely sunlight outside was drawing me out on to the fire escape. There was a cold silence that infiltrated my brain and avoided the watchtower gaze of the Numb. I felt out of my abused body. Sure I had the all too familiar markings of the day after the night before: blocked nostrils, headache and fatigue in my limbs. I did however possess clarity of thought that was fairly rare on such mornings. This was a true *reset* experience. There was a brief glimmer of hope on days such as this where you felt distant from all of the wrongdoings and free to affect a positive change.

When I was on the balcony, smoking a cigarette, the sense of calm direction intensified. It was rare to break free of the cyclical nature of my life activities but I knew today was going to be more significant than usual. It was frustrating to not know the answers to the *how, why and when* questions but this felt livable with. There was a nip in the air and as I was adorned only in a flimsy t-shirt and jeans the fresh morning breeze cut right through me. This felt appropriate though, like I was being given a mild and non-threatening dose of discomfort to wrestle with and overcome. I enjoyed seeing the billows of smoke from the now chilled depths of my lungs, a swirling, twisting grey plume that was thick and performed a belly dance for me alone. It was cool to just breathe in this chilled air. The contrast between the smoke and the light, wispy and untamable condensation of breath was beautiful and reminded me that I was truly alive.

I stubbed my cigarette out in to one of the always-overflowing ashtrays and like a thunderclap felt the cold intensify; it was like the act of smoking had distracted me from exactly how cold it was. At any rate, I needed a fizzy drink to cleanse my palette and revive my guts. As I moved towards the window, to go back inside, I felt dizzy and exhausted. I only hoped that whatever revelation was going to come to me, it came before I ran out of steam. I clambered back inside and was greeted with a waft of warm air. This felt good and immediately necessary. The foul concoction of malodorous morning stench that was created by two blokes sharing a flat was given a temporary pardon. Like the artificial smell put into noxious gases to alert their presence to any would be victim, the smell in the air of the apartment was unpleasant but alerted me to the warm, soothing airwaves it rode on. I quietly grabbed a sweater in an attempt to warm up without waking Carl. I looked over to where he was sleeping and saw an empty bed. I was going to go outside alone to see what the day would bring. I had already reconciled to myself that whatever my destiny was today it was too important to hang around the apartment while Carl took a ludicrously long time to get ready. I went to grab a soda from the fridge, cracked it open, tilted my head back and took a long draught. When my head returned to its normal position I saw Carl dressed and ready to

go, where? Who knew, but he was ready nonetheless. I felt that all the signs were pointing for me to go out, now, so I said,
"You coming"
"Yeah, just give me a second". With that he extracted a little nugget of hydro from a pocket, loaded up the pipe and took a long toke. He passed the pipe to me; I set it down straight away. I wanted to ride on the crest of my semi-clear epiphany and drug hangover buzz. It amazed me then, as it always amazed me that some people would smoke weed, mind numbing, trippy weed at that, to get straight and refresh themselves. It had the opposite effect on me; I couldn't function properly on weed. Nine out of ten times I would turn into a real space cadet, unable to perform more than the simplest tasks, like watching a movie, talking a whole load of philosophical junk, having a giggle or falling asleep.

So without any further ado it was out the apartment door, down the marble staircase; I still didn't trust the elevator, out of the two sets of doors and back into the cold. It felt like I was home again, returned to the sense of purpose I felt on the balcony, just not as safe. Stepping out on the street in New York could be an intimidating experience. You could feel like a tiny, insignificant vessel bobbing about in the vast expanse of the ocean. As I stepped out on to the street the omniscient camera, recording my life, zoomed back from me, panning further and further back, stopping at an outer space vantage point, holding still like a runner in their starting blocks, showing my thinness with anticipation, then hurtled wildly down towards me like a meteor, stopping inches from my head, bringing home the true irony of

having a soul: your life is infinitely small yet infinitely important.
So with a shake of my head I refocused and began ambling down the street.
"Thanks for waiting" bellowed Carl.
I said, "not a problem" as he caught up with me and we walked. We walked east for what seemed like ages then like a hunter on safari spotting a target I flung my arm out in Carl's way obstructing him. He gave me a funny look but I justified my irrational behavior with a point of my head and a strange excited grimace on my face. Carl looked as perplexed as I looked foolish. I craned my neck and pointed with my head again. Realizing that there was in fact no need to abandon the tried and true method of communication called talking, I gushed in a breathy, hyperventilating fashion, "look who it is".
"What, where?"
"Over there, its her. You know the funny one".
"What funny one and in any case where is the funny one anyway".
"She's fucking right there, are you blind or something" was my earnest reply. My arm was still outstretched all the way to my accusatory finger, like a riled up villager pointing out the strange one amongst them, who was in all likeliness an agent of the devil and a cat lover. This was highly embarrassing for reasons manifest. So there I was pointing at a stranger and Carl says, "why are you pointing at her, she's not doing anything funny".
"No" I exclaimed in exasperation, "it's not that she's doing something funny, she is known for being funny."
I thought that this would put Carl and me on the same page; I was sadly mistaken.

"Well if this is an example of what you find funny; a girl wearing sunglasses skulking about the place, then you should get a life. In fact I've been telling you that for ages anyway".
"Oh for fucks sake, she's not doing anything funny now, nor will she in all probability do anything funny in the next ten minutes".
"Well what makes . . ."
"What makes her funny, good question, the weed obviously hasn't slowed you down a jot, she's a fucking comedienne, a famously funny actress".
"Oh . . . Oh". Carl, with an impish look on his face entered in to the same unconvincingly covert semaphore that I had attempted to employ moments before upon first glimpse of the girl. We looked at each other and decided it was a beautiful day for a little Celebrity Safari in the wilds of the Lower East Side. It was a hunt that probably could have had us hauled up for stalking but there was no desire to actually hunt, moreover we were there as conservationists, enabling us to gather mental images of such rare specimens to recount endlessly to anyone who would listen. The interest was usually quite high mid way through getting quite high.
We followed the incognito ingénue for a couple of blocks, but as we went further into Alphabet City the smell of patchouli oil and a host of other incense sticks burning started to nauseate me. So I suggested to Carl we break away from this temporary diversion and find something better to do. The only problem with this was that the daytime was not our forte and we didn't really know what one was expected to do.
I suggested we venture into a cool looking dingy boutique that was called something like the Cat

The Numb and Me and Green Trainers

and the Moon. The area was rife with places named after celestial bodies and mundane earthly things or animals. I wouldn't be surprised if there was a 'Sun and Corkscrew' or 'Venus and her Penguins'. So we went in and were greeted by a funky looking late teenage girl with pigtails, black thick-rimmed glasses, a mini skirt, fish net stockings and knee length boots that if described as chunky would be like describing an atom as little. She wore black lipstick and black painted fingernails with a silver jewelry adorning her fingers as well as her eyebrow and tongue. The overriding experience I got from being in close proximity to this gothic princess was the distinct smell of fabric softener, which reminded me of home and endeared me to her.

She on the other hand wanted no endearing of mine at all and curtly said, "Can I help you, 'cos standing room in here is for customers only".

I was slightly distressed by this not because it burst my patronizing bubble about not to judge a book by its cover, and how all walks of life like their clothes soft etc. But, because I had no idea what this shop sold and if there was in fact anything I would be tempted to spend my drugs money on. The place turned out to sell coffee and innumerable teas. After what seemed like solving the riddle of the sphinx I was brought a cup of English Breakfast tea. I had got used to and in fact fell in love with many facets of American life but having a tea bag left dangling on the end of a piece of string, in turn stapled to a small piece of cheap looking paper advertising the brand, was always horrible. It always tasted like shit too. You may well ask why I didn't venture into the exotic world of their many hand-blended teas from far and wide. The answer lies in the fact that I was out of my element, in the daylight and just wanted a cuppa.

I ordered my tea, no flirting allowed, and was immediately prompted to part with three bucks fifty. After tax and a grudgingly given tip, this was close to five. I commented, "Wow, great value as well as impeccable service". My comments were drowned out by the frothing of milk and garnered no response; this was just as well.

If I had been paying for this most expensive of hand picked tea, all the way from India via London, by how hot it was it would have been a bargain. I lowered my mouth to the mug and dunked my top lip in to the liquid without a care. Fractions of a second later I jerked the scalding liquid away from my scalded lip and inadvertently sloshed some on to my inner thigh. I scanned the room at the same time as letting out a half roar half yelp kind of noise. Within seconds the nuclear reaction in my groin subsided to leave just a damp patch irritating the prickly scorched skin underneath. This whole episode was luckily not witnessed by anyone. The Goth barista was fiddling around with the coffee machine; maybe cleaning it or just avoiding having to have any further contact with me; and Carl was in outer space somewhere. I spontaneously raised the super heated tea to my mouth again; looked into the half empty mug and shook my head slowly from side to side as if to say 'you're not gonna get me again'; and conceded defeat. I placed the tea back on the table. Carl said,

"Are you done?"

Yes I was done.

I stood up uneasily in a bow legged fashion and attempted to sneak out of the door unnoticed. The girl

The Numb and Me and Green Trainers

behind the counter craned her neck round and gave me a half smile that felt more like an 'I hate you' than a belated come on. My eyebrows raised and my eyes widened as if being controlled by a third party. I opened the shop door still mulling over what this smile could mean when the girl broke the mystery and turned and walked away.

This was a really unfortunate turn of events not just for all the obvious reasons. This little event really broke the flow of the meandering morning. All things, even as vague as they were, felt like they were following the right path. But that smile. That smile had thrown a cat amongst the pigeons. That moment of uncertainty summoned forth the Numb. I knew now that any sense of fate or karma was out of the window today. My old pal would guide the day toward an unknown and almost certainly weighty conclusion.

Carl's buzz was wearing off and I needed him to be at least partially stoned for the rest of the day or until such time as the Numb revealed his hand. I suggested we went back to the apartment for a little pick me up, Carl agreed so off we went. It was no more than a twenty minute walk from where we were in the East village to the apartment. The beauty of Manhattan was that once you had learnt the layout of downtown and the simple grid system above First Street it was pretty easy to navigate your way around and judge walking times. We had to go about ten streets up and four avenues over. The walk could have been achieved in several ways, but I knew that my feet were being guided; I was being led. Once you were out of the Village, either East or West, the city adopted a more formal role again. So, it surprised me to find myself walking down a street past

several funky looking kids who were unmistakably art students of some description. I asked Carl if he knew the score. Like a town crier making a grand announcement, he immediately started rattling off information about the famous institution we were standing outside of. Like a Geiger counter detecting a huge quake the numb rattled inside me with excitement and anticipation. This was it.
I said to Carl,
"I'm going in ok"
"But you don't have an appointment or . . ."
"I'll see you in a little while"
I read the plaque outside the building; "The Acting Institute" then opened the heavy black door.
It's strange how things work out. Here I was full of adrenalin in a really controlled environment. There was a palpable feeling of artiness with cool looking kids milling around. To clarify the 'controlled' bit: five minutes prior to standing in the Institute I was ambling around the East Village in a seemingly pointless fashion. There were no rules or direction other than the pull of inevitability that got me to where I was standing. Inside the building there was a clear purpose in the behavior of the other people. The feel of the place was a lot less starched and stiff than the Academy; the students seemed more relaxed, well as relaxed as highly strung actor types can get, there was also an absence of security personnel at the door which de-institutionalized the place. The kids in the entry hall all seemed to be moving in chaotic unison. Although they all appeared to be doing there own thing there was a commonality in the pace of their movements, like separate waves joined by their purpose as the incoming tide. I had experienced being

out of sync before and here I felt it again. My body was an interesting lump of contradictions. I felt heavy and weightless at the same time as if I was experiencing a space walk. I was so nervous and excited about stepping forward into the unknown that my heart was being red lined but at the same time I was calm, focused and felt safe and protected.

I scanned the walls that were peppered with notice boards and headshots of a variety of famous actors that had attended this place. The Academy had the same idea of advertising the dream of success, fame and fortune but there it seemed forced, like prize pedigrees that were being shown off in a rather clipped and distant fashion. Here the cheesy mug shots seemed like part of the furniture. This perception may well have just been governed by the excitement of the situation but there was something in the air here that just felt right. I began looking more intently at the notice board. There were pages of A4 paper with quickly scrawled advertisements at the top of them with their ubiquitous tasseled bottoms inviting you to pull of a strip of paper with the number to call if you were interested in the product. The two things that were always being advertised were second-hand futons and vacancies for a place to stay, both obviously at exorbitant prices. There were a few flyers for music gigs and shows to go to if you were interested in supporting your peers. I generally hadn't been up to until this point but who knew what the future would bring.

It never occurred to me that I was probably trespassing and not really eligible to be eying up the prize finds and pine furniture bargains on display. I was just going about my business taking things as they came. After a little while a cold feeling came over me like someone 'walking on my grave' as my old man would say. I turned my head to see a congregation of four people, one of which was looking me up and down, unfortunately not in an approving way. I felt that I had been discovered as a spy, an outsider. Before my brain could engage properly I felt myself lurching towards a heavily made up pale-faced girl.

"Office" I said in a dream like state.

"'Scuse me" was the reply in an Americanized eastern European accent.

"I wonder . . ." I refused to look down; I knew the green trainers would be there. I felt cold and obsolete.

By this stage the other people in the group were dismissively looking in my direction. I quickly looked at each of them when the pale girl said,

"Yes" in a neutral but inquisitive way. I was stunned like a deer in headlights but fought through and asked,

"Can you tell me where the admissions office is . . . please?" I was hoping that the girl would warm to me now I found the ability to string enough words together to form a sentence. I was hoping for a moment like the ones you see in the romantic comedy films where the once cold and disinterested party softens to the idiot who is embarrassing himself and usually with a cutesy cock of the head and toothy smile points the hapless one in the right direction. This is usually followed by a quick guilty look over the shoulder to see the new romantic interest walking in to something or someone, dropping something or generally making an arse of him or herself. The intrigued stranger then shakes their head and smiles as if to say 'There's just something about . . .' the general spacing out is promptly interrupted by one of the group and the fledgling lover is brought back down to earth.

So there I was smiling to myself when I was interrupted by an abrupt grunt,

"Over there", she pointed with her head then immediately went back to her conversation. I started to say thanks but lost interest half way through and walked about ten steps to an open door that was clearly marked as the office. Inside there were three desks each with the usual office clutter: computers, telephones etc. Two of the desks had people sitting behind them. There was one man with a beard and a kind smile and a woman in her late forties who looked like how you would imagine 'mother of the year' to look. She again had a very kind face with a warm smile and understanding eyes. So there I was in the doorway commanding the attention of both people in the office and this time was not lost for words. Like a runner out of the blocks I hurriedly asked,

"Can I speak to someone about joining the school". The man with the beard looked over at the woman and subsequently so did I. She introduced herself as Elaine and introduced me to her colleague John. I felt like I was being reunited with long lost family. I was really impressed that the two faculty introduced themselves by their first names, again it just felt right; thousands of miles away from home living a very alternative lifestyle the last thing you need is to be patronized and made to feel like a child at school. Elaine stood up and didn't appear much taller than when she was sitting down, she offered her hand out to me and said,

"And you are?"

She led me to a little office just around the corner and just as she was closing the door behind us a little dog bolted past us and out the door. I clearly looked a little perplexed not just by seeing a dog here, which was weird in its own right, but by seeing an animal at all. It struck me that it had been a while since I could remember seeing an animal. There are obviously animals to be seen in New York: the zoo, Uptown near the park and the West Village, but also, this city was festooned with critters who occupied every nook and cranny neglected by the human animals, dire and pathetic, existing on the detritus and scum of the creatures that society deemed more wholesome. Anyway, I spent little to no time in any of these places on a regular basis.

Elaine explained that the little fur ball was in fact her dog and was part of the furniture. I accepted this straight away and as we sat down to begin talking something rather strange happened. Elaine gestured towards a seat for me then moved towards a chair for her just opposite in this rather closet like room. I was just preparing myself to sit when Elaine came hurtling towards me. In fairness she was falling towards the floor and I just happened to be in the way. As Elaine was taking the couple of steps towards her seat she had not seen a small pool left by her charming little fur ball. She slipped in the dog piss and began falling backwards. I was just in the right place at the right time I guess. I was a little dismayed at the way things were panning out. I was cradling the Head of Admissions for a really well known and desirable acting school in my arms. I looked down at her rosy red face and got the impression that Elaine was not so much embarrassed but entertained by the events. She raised her eyebrows as if to say 'oh

The Numb and Me and Green Trainers

well, isn't this just swell'. The interesting thing about this incident was that it completely broke the ice. As I began to prop Elaine back into the upright position there was a very domestic, unglamorous and unpretentious air in the room. We looked at each other with a spontaneous excitement that seemed natural and soft edged. Elaine broke her smiling gaze to look at the small puddle on the ground and said,
"Oh, Henry . . . Henry, Henry, Henry."
I hoped she was not addressing me as part of some kind of impromptu acting exercise.
"He's usually so good."
I rolled my eyes and gently shook my head from side to side. This was my way of sitting on the fence. I neither wanted to be a serious grump about what her little dog had done nor did I want to play the incident down just in case Elaine was concerned about the out of character behavior. Either way the dog had done me a favor and engendered my non-committal reaction as a reward. I was feeling a little uncomfortable by the slick of urine that was being ignored by Elaine but without Henry's intervention, who knows how things would have turned out? Maybe the focus would have been how burnt out, unkempt and empty I was. Maybe I would have been faced with a barrage of questions about the science of acting and my role in it. I shook these thoughts out of my head and realized I was staring at Elaine's legs. She had sat down knees tight together with her legs snugly tucked under her chair. This body language seemed to make the room feel even smaller. The floor space was now effectively a no man's land with two pairs of feet and legs jostling for room. Elaine took in a deep breath and my eyes snapped up to meet hers. She was wearing

a half smile on her face but her eyes were beaming a bright content smile acknowledging me as the hero of the hour; saving her tailbone from a beating. As she breathed out she began looking at me quizzically. I felt a wave of panic wash over me. The reality of the situation struck me for the first time since I woke up. Here I was without a plan or any real desire to be anywhere outside of my drug addled existence about to face a serious interview by someone who does this type of thing for a living. The arrogance that was me; I mean, how dare I come in here and waste this person's time? Who was I to turn up on a whim, be involved in a rather slapstick incident and then bugger off just because I felt drawn here in the midst of a quasi-psychotic hangover? I was getting my second wind of adrenalin and knew this would be the last burst of natural energy I would feel today. I felt like a churlish schoolboy who was just about to get rumbled on an extravagant deception but to my surprise Elaine's examining look melted away and a little voice inside my head echoed, 'too close'.

The questions did eventually start to pour out from Elaine's relaxed mouth. There was something quite therapeutic answering questions that were designed to cut to the heart of one's perceptions and intentions when you really hadn't a clue about how you felt about anything. Unintentionally this interview was a true test of natural acting talent and in that I mean lying convincingly. The questions were along the lines of: What do you feel you could contribute to the Institute? How do you feel the Institute can contribute to your growth as an actor and a person?

As you can see there was a great deal of emphasis placed upon contributions of which I could only offer my wisp-like ungrounded insincerity. The only tangible contribution I could make, I was very generous in freely donating: my parents hard earned money. The school was expensive especially for International students but hey what's another couple of thousand when you were having this much fun. Although I didn't know it at the time I needed a way of staying in New York. That was the pressing feeling that churned inside me. That was what forced me through the doors and in to the room with Elaine. The other focus of the questions was of course The Institute. I was having my brain picked in such a way as to suggest that other students had given some premeditated thought into attending the place and not just walked in off the street. I was not here to take the piss out of Elaine or the Institute; the place felt good, cool and welcoming in a way the Academy never did; but the constant references to the methodology of the place coupled with name checking the founder every sentence made it feel like you were being recruited into a cult. The way the questions were loaded it was as if you would be absolved of any past indiscretions both in the world of acting and life in general once you had been baptized and pledged into the flock. This was meaningless in one way but interestingly poignant in another. I had given no special thought, in fact no thought at all, to the workings or existence of the Institute before this point but somehow the answers that I was giving were hitting all the right notes. I maintain that however random the events were that led me to this strange interview there was nothing vague about the experience. I was answering the questions that were being put to me concerning the Institute with a mix of global answers reflecting my worldview and my subconscious thoughts. Except for the absence of a comfortable chair to relax into I was in fact in a therapy session. This was a golden opportunity to wash myself clean of the head funk that I had been building up that was slowly melting my feeling of self-worth and belief that the world could breath clean air again. As I answered the questions I got on a bit of a roll. I substituted my hopes and dreams about the future of humanity with the specific questions about acting and the Institute. For instance my answer to the question about what I could contribute to the Institute basically was my dream about how the perfect me would act in a perfect world. There was lots of talk about dedication to achieve one's goals, single-mindedness only in a good way repackaged as ambition but obviously not at the expense of others etc. The answers to the questions about what the Institute could do for me were a little harder to answer for obvious reasons but I applied the same tactic as before. I substituted what I would want a best friend or mentor to teach me about life, replaced the mentor with the word Institute and life with the word acting. Things were going really well. I was rattling off answers to all the questions with the gusto of a cocaine conversation unhindered by sobriety. One of the things you hear a lot is how boring people are when they are loaded on coke. I do wonder how much of the reaction is a form of personal censorship; not wanting to tolerate a moment of somebody who is desperately trying to figure out what ever it is before he forgets or lets go of the rocket ship, scared that some sense may emerge from the mouth of a druggy in amongst the self indulgent bullshit. The lack of empathy for people who get high by people who get drunk is fascinatingly cruel but very telling of who needs to stay within the lines of life's coloring book.

Well time to put the soapbox away for a little while and back to the interview.

I was doing well in the interview by being honest. Maybe not honest in the conventional meaning of telling the truth but my truth was being honored. I had something to say about how I felt about the world and how I fitted in and as the questions came up I saw a way of feeling relevant and refreshed. Without the 'catch the falling person' trust exercise that happened at the top of the interview things may have been different but they weren't. Right from the get go Elaine had a twinkle in her eye that reassured me and by the end of our time together I felt quietly confident of being offered a place in the old hallowed halls of the Institute. I offered my hand to Elaine, which was duly shaken, and she led me out in to the hallway. I felt a little uncomfortable in saying goodbye. I felt really at home there as if by my purging in the interview room I had somehow formed a real bond with the place unlike anything I had felt in a while. As slowly as possible I walked down the short corridor to the exit looking at the notice boards with less guilty eyes now feeling a little more entitled to the glance at the valuable but treasure less ads. As I got to the heavy door I peaked over my shoulder but there was no one there so I nodded a thank you to the empty hallway then proceeded out.

The sun dazzled my eyes and I squinted and held my hand up to my face. I could see the blurred outlines of a few people and could smell cigarette smoke and the inescapable Manhattan odor on the slight breeze. I rather enjoyed a few seconds of relying on a sense other than sight to be my principle guide but equally relished having things come back into focus. To my surprise one of the blurry figures was none other than Carl. I was pleased if not a little perplexed to see him still there bearing in mind that the apartment was near by; one of the benefits of a morning spliff I thought to myself as Carl clearly had no idea of how long I'd been gone. He drew a cigarette out of a pack and handed it to me. I placed it in my dry lips and reached in to my pockets for a light; no need; Carl produced a match and said "Well . . . ?"

We walked back to Carl's apartment briskly as if marching towards purpose even though we weren't. I was loathed to go into the specifics of the interview at the Institute. Carl knew a fair bit about the acting world in New York, far more than me, which was sometimes interesting but mainly irksome. It comes back to that insecure tendency of the rebel to not be alone in rebellion. It was one thing to strike out at the world and behave in a contrary way but to have a fully committed accomplice enabled the good times to roll and huge amounts of guilt to roll off your back. Carl's knowledge of the acting world rubbed up against his recklessness and caused unnecessary friction. You want your baddies to be really bad not bad only in between pockets of good behavior. I remembered how it felt to be back at school, way back at the Comp, talking to some of the mischievous mates about how you hadn't done your homework or hadn't known about or prepared for a test only to find that you were in fact alone in your defiance feeling really let down and sold out. So there were a couple of reasons I kept quiet when Carl was earnestly asking about how it went with the interview.

The Numb and Me and Green Trainers

One: territorial pissing pure and simple. For once I knew something that Carl didn't and wanted it to stay that way and two: I had staked a claim to something potentially good and productive and didn't want it sullied by my other life. It didn't occur to me that eventually the two worlds would have to collide but this was a good thing for now.

I arrived back at the apartment with Carl and immediately grimaced at the stench of the place as we walked in. The air was still thick with morning body stink and was not helped by the pungent aroma of cashed pipes and extinguished joints. Maybe my morning mission of unusual productivity had ushered into me a newfound piety. I thought this was unlikely but did appeal to Carl to give the place a little spring clean. I knew I should have been tired and jonesing for some drugs but for whatever reason I wasn't. I just wanted the place to feel a little more wholesome. With the apartment in such a state of disarray I didn't know where to start but felt that it was a two-man job. I looked over at Carl ready to ask him what he wanted to do but ended up shaking my head from side to side with affectionate disapproval as he had brought out the big bong. He was standing over the long functional glass chamber drawing as much smoke in to the waiting room as possible. You could always tell whether someone was really going for a big hit by the density of the smoke in the cylinder and looking at the state of the bong Carl was glued to I realized I would be cleaning alone. This kind of suited me and I racked my brain deciding where to start. Carl let out a guttural sound that was half choking half sighing and a plume of sweet marijuana smoke filled the room. I couldn't really smell the grizzly funk anymore, I must have acclimatized to it, but I opened the window anyway to see if I could renew the sense of disgust that hit me on arrival. Fresh air trickled in and danced around with the cumulative bad smells but seemed to exacerbate them rather than water them down. One minute you would get hit by cool fresh air and take in a deep breath only to inhale a rather less appetizing lungful. The temperature of the room had plummeted and gave a real argument to how smelly was better than chilly. I rushed over to the window and closed it. This felt like sealing a tomb; it was unlikely that we would venture out again so the fresh air that was inside was all we would be getting for the foreseeable future. I looked over at Carl who was shuffling some old pizza boxes around with no clear direction or coordination. He was clearly doing his bit to tidy up but I felt uninspired now. The radiators were slowly warming the room back up and without realizing it I was now sitting down on the couch. I put my head back, then silence.

I was walking down a corridor with doors on either side of me. The narrow channel seemed to go on for about twenty feet in front of me and as I turned around I could see the corridor spiking out endlessly to a far away vanishing point. I tried to take a step backwards but my body would not cooperate. I willed my body backwards but nothing. I became aware of the silence of the sliver of a room and felt unsettled. I closed my eyes, held my breath and with gritted teeth urged myself backwards. I felt cold and was rushing now; the counter balance to the calm I felt whilst flying down the icy mountain a few years ago. I felt anxious and nauseous as the bitterly cold wind was stinging my knuckles and ears. I was falling straight down now as if plummeting towards oblivion on

The Numb and Me and Green Trainers

a terminal sky dive. The force of the wind against my body had arched my back to breaking point and horror filled me to the arterioles as I caught a first glimpse of the ground coming rushing towards me. I tried to put my arms out to in a desperate attempt to break my fall but they were forced back and immovable. A deafening clanging that could not be shut out broke the silence. The god of war spitefully struck the embittered steel as he forged the weapons of Armageddon. Bang; the metallic pounding continued. Bang, bang, bang. I could no longer tell where the cacophony stopped and my heartbeat began. The noise had completely taken over and dehumanized me. I was now faceless as I was being absorbed into the maelstrom. The ground was nearly upon me now as I began to come undone. I was being stripped back at a molecular level. I was dematerializing, ceasing to exist as if passing through an event horizon. By the time I was due to make my last collision there was nothing left of me but a single unidentifiable thought, a hint of life with no remaining fingerprints. The noise had stopped. Then there was gravity again. I could feel the outlines of my body and a slow rhythmic drumbeat that slowly fleshed out to a heartbeat. I opened my eyes. I was in the narrow corridor again facing forwards with doors on either side of me. Hanging from the doors there were now flashing neon signs. I craned my neck round to see the infinite corridor behind me and knew more now than when I had first looked back. I turned my head forwards and proceeded to investigate the neon signs. I couldn't decipher the words on the doors but as I inched nearer to the signs I could feel a magnetic pull or repulsion. I attempted to open the doors that beckoned me on but none of them would budge. I forced myself towards the doors that were resisting my investigation and those would not open. I was getting increasingly agitated and started thrashing out kicking the doors and pounding on them with my fists. I got to the end of the corridor and saw a small red button behind a breakable piece of glass. There was no instruction or warning just the button. I attempted to go backwards but couldn't and got an overwhelming sense that it was better not to try. So there was nothing left except the red button and me. I knew by the way things were going that there were no real choices in this corridor just forced directions and confusing irritating riddles. I shook my head knowing that pressing the button was not a matter of choice but rather inevitability and without any further hesitation punched the glass. I heard a whirring noise behind me and turned to see the neon signs on the doors start to spin round. Letters and numbers flickered on the doors like the big departure signs at train station. The bright colorful letters and the hypnotic whirring sound temporarily mesmerized me but the spell was broken as a decipherable letter emerged on the left side of the door.

L.

There was still a flurry of color as random figures spun round as if on the wheels of a one-arm bandit. Next to the still 'L' on the door a further shape emerged and came to a resting position. It was another letter,

I.

Then another letter,

F.

The whirring had died down to a faint hum and it became clear that there was only room left on the doors for one more letter. Seconds later the last spinning figure came to rest. It was the letter,

E.

All of the doors as far as you could see presented the same four letters 'LIFE'.

"Wonderful" I said out loud to the empty corridor.

It was obvious what the point to this little charade was and I said,

"OK, very poignant but what the fuck do you want me to do about it you miserable bastard?"

No response. I heard a click from in front of me as if a latch had been released and turned forward. The red button had gone and in its place was an ornate brass door handle. On the floor there was a doormat with the words 'Home Sweet Home' on it. I reached for the handle and unlike the other doors in the corridor this one gave off no vibrations at all. The handle was cold and heavy and as I depressed it an outline of a door formed then creaked open. I pushed forward and entered the space beyond the door. I was standing in darkness that turned pitch black as the door closed and the corridor became nothing more than a memory.

I felt an ease of movement in this seemingly cavernous space. There was no direction or plan, no feeling. I thought that I was afraid of the dark but here, wherever here is or was, there was no emotion or trace of feeling alive. I saw a green light flicker in the distance and squinted towards it. Above me I heard a whisper "Home". I looked up but saw nothing but darkness. Seconds later I looked down and standing right in front of me there was a cloaked figure illuminated only by the flickering green light of a jet black candle. I now knew who had ushered me into his domain. He had never infiltrated me this deeply before. He had never shown himself before. I looked down and was naked in front of the cloaked figure bar all too familiar footwear.

The figure in front of me dropped the candle to reveal matching green trainers. The flickering flame caught on the cloak of my host and set him ablaze with an immolating blast. He reached out to me and I took his hand with no fear. The flames spread to me and initially were unfelt. Then a prickly tingle spread over me as the green flames licked and probed my naked flesh. The tingling became more fierce and started to burn. My insides felt that they were burning and my mouth was full of flames. An agonizing pain bent me in half and I looked up towards the Numb and screamed,

"Home!"

I sprung up patting myself down. I was in Carl's apartment dripping with sweat, my skin tingling. I saw Carl and said to him "Home". He raised his eyebrows and nodded his head slowly acknowledging that this was my home and said,

"I don't think you're alright. I think we need to get you something to take the edge off."

I looked at him with a blank expression.

"Have I been sleeping?"

"Dunno, maybe, don't think so" was the response with the clarity of mud. Carl continued, "even for an insomniac I wouldn't consider closing your eyes for a few seconds sleeping."

"But there was a corridor, I couldn't go back and then I saw . . . ."

'Go on tell him' rang out in my head.

" . . . nothing, Carl."

Carl looked at me strangely.

I looked forwards blankly feeling bewildered but defiant and said, "did you say something about taking the edge off?"

Of course the edge was never taken off. I would simply plaster over the cracks in an attempt to hide the jagged edges. The efforts to hide the pointy bits were badly covered up. In many situations I was left with an unconvincing layering of misfortune that could be read by anyone with even a modicum of common sense. One need not appreciate nuance to see what is in front of them; in the same way someone could see a dissected portion of tree and see the rings, even counting them and feign knowledge about what it all means, holding no real understanding. There is however observation and recognition without understanding.

Another restless night, couldn't tell whether it was the desolate host willingly received all night or my conscience that set the fever in, but the fever was in and it took a mighty grip of me. I writhed in the bed sheets rocking my head from one side to the other in the vain attempt to find a comfortable spot. But my neck was so stiff. My head was drenched and any movement just seemed to dampen the pillow and surrounding area. This all compounded the nuisance of restlessness and I wished for calm. There was no calm to be had here though. Here I couldn't stretch a fleshy patch over the gape in my soul, I was laid bare. There was no way to slow myself down: the breathing was furiously erratic, legs twitched, beads of sweat rushed down my neck and shins. I longed for a gust of cooling air to take away some of the discomfort. This fresh breeze that I would allow in quickly turned to icy fingers freezing the rivers of sweat on my body. No escape from the busy discomfort that separates the good in us from the survival instincts. Although the room was quiet and still, the inner turbulence brought with it a noise enough to keep my nerves shredded. There was something loud about being so restless and desperate. The city outside the window seemed to breath in sympathy of me as it watched on humming its night music. I scrunched my eyes up tight and placed my forearms over my face and enjoyed a second of calm before a shiver ran down my body and I descended once more in to despair. This night was not dissimilar to many others but this offered no consolation, the bodily sensations and the spinning brain always felt immediate and overpowering. By the time dawn started to break the fury of the nights restlessness had given way to a really heavy limbed tiredness. I was still alert but stiff and achy at the same time. As dawn gave way to morning it became clear that the opportunity to sleep had gone forever. The fever of the night had been broken so too had the paralyzing head-spin that made thinking clearly or concentrating impossible. As I regained the ability to worry about things I briefly scanned over the terrain of my life and shook my head from side to side, wide eyed with eyebrows raised. But that was it for remorse and worrying. For now, that's all I had the capacity to give.

I hadn't given much thought to the meeting at the Institute since sauntering in and having my interview. The event had become another loose memory. One casual day a couple of weeks after my chance meeting at the Institute a letter arrived. I opened the letter to read that I had indeed been given a place at the Institute if I wanted it. This event seemed on script and certainly a good excuse to fire up the party. There were some true emotions to be had here but they were so watered down and lost in the conflict of numbness and feeling something, like a hand searching in the dark trying to find a pulse, that artificial feeling dominated like a limp-wristed despot with green blood pumping through his veins.

There was a month to kill before the start of classes at the Institute and I had nothing to do now but wait. Wait with increasing anxiety as I approached yet another blank slate, unblemished and wholesome; well at least in comparison to the mess I made of everything. I was like a painter trying to keep a room immaculately whitewashed whilst wearing wet paint splashed overalls. The sense of trepidation I had in regards to attending the Institute was spiked by the possibility of success. This gave me the chance once again, to break away from the decayed partial life that had become the norm. I reflected on the present and the future, I interlaced potentially interchangeable circumstances, both real but slippery and hard to hold on to.

Things were changing; my strange friend was nowhere to be seen, not taunting or seething in its usual fashion. The majesty of New York City had reached its zenith and finally I was ready to venture out into the anti-city. I was off to a house party in Jersey City with a new pal who ensured me that life began as you were engulfed deeper and deeper in the PATH tunnel.

Terry was a handsome man standing sinewy at six-foot-three with a surf of curly blond hair. Terry scared and excited me with equal voracity. My birthday, the denouement of this adventure, was shadowed with the specter of 'the tuck'. I was dreading the revelation of this unusual birthday dark-treat and I sensed that it would involve pain and suffering like being jumped-in, again; but Terry wasn't going to let me off the hook. After all the anticipation and a couple of gas-mask bong hits with Bacardi 151 tube liquor, courtesy of Terry's friend Charley, a ripped statuesque figure sprung naked out of the doorway with his cock and balls tucked between his crossed legs. It was like a bizarre hermaphrodite-fallen-angel mark of ambiguity. I'd worried about nothing and felt real relief after such apprehension.

The Numb would have been on red alert if anything was untoward; my green shadow would never place me in harms way.

So we left for the party and with a bottle of Everclear still dressed in its brown paper as our companion, I knew the night could only get better.

Things were cooling down and looking up . . .

Epilogue

Some people say home is where the heart is, working on the rather dubious notion we know our decrepit cancer riddled blood pumps.
And where's home?
A place to lay your cap, that's been pinching the circumference of your dome all day. The unsightly indentation leaves not particularly rugged uniformed marks that look adolescent at best and a million miles from the designer Wartime pilots' hair lined scars of a bygone age.
Solace is found in my slightly malodorous but wonderful Homeys'. These slippers are the herringbone pair 'cos my socks today are thin. The dilapidated grey slippers are a must if the thick wool jacquard socks make an appearance.
My ankles are swollen and my balance now leaves a lot to be desired so the routine of disrobing can be super fun. I finally am left with the crumpled innards of my jeans looking abused on the floor. The seams are representative of a pretzel and I've lost both slippers and a sock in the process. My only solace is that this farce is common and true.

Unable to get to the worst itch, the Numb is venom: disgusting and vindictive; even the most ardent legion

of voices metamorphoses into something better in a bad universe, for it is hard to be truly rotten.
Cruelty and selfishness are now who I am. They attempt to defibrillate the necrotic flesh with labels of schizophrenia and psycho effective disorder and borderline personality disorder but these baselines are nearly unknowable and imperceptible as the balmy salve of something less than decency soothes the last vestiges of my faith. The choirs' Endeavour's, floating on the cold light air, remind me of the polish and venire, the seduction of the established order, so I press on alone.

I am the lost, the unforgivable and my restless journey edges closer to my Tartarus.

So Home . . . It's the anti Numb.
The world is where we find a home.
This is the endeavor of love and peace even in the language of vitriol.

About The Author

Euan is thirty three and is married with twins. He has lived in both coasts of America, London and now Canterbury in the South East of the UK.